D0681505

"CHRISTIAN WOODVILLE—
THE ONLY TIME HE EVER
DEIGNED TO LOOK AT ME,
HE TOLD ME THAT I
PAINTED LIKE A MAN!"

*But she was definitely a
woman—as Christian was
soon to discover. . . .*

Also by Rebecca Baldwin
and available from Fawcett Books:

A GENTLEMAN FROM PHILADELPHIA

THE CASSANDRA KNOT

THE MATCHMAKERS

A NOVEL BY

Rebecca Baldwin

FAWCETT COVENTRY • NEW YORK

THE MATCHMAKERS

Published by Fawcett Coventry Books, a unit of CBS Publications, the Consumer Publishing Division of CBS Inc.

Copyright © 1980 by Rebecca Baldwin

ALL RIGHTS RESERVED

ISBN: 0-449-50017-9

Printed in the United States of America

First Fawcett Coventry printing: January 1980

10 9 8 7 6 5 4 3 2 1

To the Henry and Reilly Show

THE MATCHMAKERS

Chapter One

The brass knocker at Number 16, Upper Mount Street did not have to fall twice before Coe, the second footman, had jumped up from his chair to attend to the opening of that fashionable portal.

The gentleman who stood upon the step, hat and walking stick under one arm of his finely cut coat of Wellington superfine, was a vision of sartorial splendor from his carefully brushed and pomaded brown locks to his burnished Hessians.

Coe, who possessed modest ambitions to attain someday the lofty rank of gentleman's gentleman, respectfully stepped aside to allow the gentleman entry, carefully studying the exquisite folds of his snowy cravat as he relieved the visitor of his high-crowned beaver, his famous silver-headed stick and a pair of buff gloves of softest leather. "Day, Coe," the gentleman drawled, casting an approving eye over his own reflection in the gilded mirror. "I trust her ladyship's in the green salon as usual?"

Before Coe could reply, Basile, the august butler, alerted by some sixth sense to the presence of "a presence" abovestairs, had swept majestically into the hallway.

"Good day, Lord Brandamore," he said in his funereal accents, long familarity in no way diminishing his own role.

Brandamore, reluctantly tearing his gaze away from his own reflection, gave the slightest twist to his neck gear and nodded. "Ah, Basile. Tell me, is she in the devil's own taking? Know I'm an hour late, but my man and I simply could not achieve the right effect with my shirt points this morning. Daresay we ran through twenty collars before we settled upon this one." He shrugged.

"And very elegant, if I may say so," Basile allowed himself to comment soothingly as he led his lordship toward the rear apartments with a stately tread. "If I may make so bold as to inform your lordship, Lady Charlotte has been closeted with her mantua maker most of the morning. I believe this person has distracted her attention from the time."

Brandamore, sauntering along behind the butler, nodded. "Female comin' into colors again's got to look her best," he observed cheerfully. "Is Woodville about?"

"No, my lord. I believe Mr. Woodville has gone to attend an auction of Italian watercolors at Christie's," Basile informed the visitor.

"Good," Lord Brandamore said simply.

Basile, who was fully aware of the antipathy his master bore his stepmother's chief *cicerone*, merely threw open the double doors of the green salon, announcing, "Lord Brandamore, my lady!"

My lady was seated upon a brocade sofa of gray and green stripe, surrounded by a profusion of laces and silks, a fashion journal open upon her lap. In the gray and white round gown and buffeted morning cap considered proper for a widow just emerging from her mourning period, she looked younger than her twenty years. The piquancy of her young widowhood was increased by the delicate tendrils of ashen blond hair peeking out from the lace border of her morning cap, framing a face of exquisitely delicate beauty. A pair of enormous blue eyes, framed by dark lashes that owed something to the skill of her dresser's dye-pots, surveyed her old friend with anguish. "George!" She cried out in her shimmering, breathless voice, "How am I to chose between the pointe-pois and the Venice silk?" She waved two swatches of spidery lace toward him in agonies of indecision.

As Basile closed the doors upon these two old friends, Brandamore unceremoniously removed a small ball of silky fur from a chair nearest the hearth and seated himself in lazy elegancy, carefully stretching out his long, buckskin-breeched legs toward the grate. He raised his quizzing glass toward the outstretched hands and studied the two bits of fabric critically. "Venice silk!" he declared at last. "Pointe-pois would only make you look like a dowd. Saw Sally Jersey wearin' it at the opera last night and told her the same thing."

There were those who said that Lady Charlotte Woodville's intelligence was as minimal as her heart was large, but no one could contest her leadership in society. Not even her loss of the late Vincent Woodville, a gentleman more than twice her age who had been borne off in an unfortunate bout of the influenza, and her subsequent mourning period, could quite diminish the subtle, if sometimes ruthless, power Lady Charlotte held over the Upper Ten Thousand. The acquisition of this power could best be explained by the fortunate circumstance of her being the favorite cousin of Lord Brandamore (perhaps because their connection was so distant) and the wife of Mr. Woodville, one of the warmest men in London. But mere money was not enough; for Brandamore, it was only a tool—a most necessary tool—in the development of style. And for Lord Brandamore, style was everything.

Whatever else one could say about Lord Brandamore—and there were those who could say much—he was definitely the social arbiter of the ton. Since poor Mr. Brummell's star had been so unfortunately eclipsed, Lord Brandamore's had risen on the horizon. The publication of his romantic poems, by Newfield in three leatherbound volumes, had served to cast almost every female heart in the metropolis at his gleaming boots quite soon upon his coming down from Magdalen College; his sartorial display was such that a lifted eyebrow had been enough to destroy the vogue for jeweled stickpins overnight; no party was considered truly tonnish without one of his brief appearances. A natural wit had been honed by a cynical observation of the world and its follies to a razor's edge. Nothing amused him more than the status society had chosen to bestow upon him, unless it was the use of that status to send all of them scrambling to imitate one of his latest fancies or abjure one of his latest pets. And in this respect, as in all others since their cradle days, he was ably assisted by his cousin Lady Charlotte.

As a beautiful debutante endowed with only a modest dowry, as well as several hopeful brothers and sisters, she had been firmly brought up by her mama to "make a good match." Cynical though Brandamore might be, he also realized that it was in his best interests to be sure that

Charlotte married well enough to keep her sib-
lings from applying to him for further assistance;
and he had gently but firmly guided her eyes
away from several very romantic and dashing
younger men of lesser means and persuaded her
to accept the hand of Sir Vincent Woodville,
a gentleman past his forty-fifth birthday with a
son only seven years Charlotte's senior. To Brandamore's credit, Sir Vincent had been a handsome and sophisticated man who plainly adored
and indulged his young and foolish wife, and for
a female raised up without a father since the age
of ten, the image presented by her husband's
subtle bridle and devotion was enough to win
over her rather shallow affections.

It was generally accepted that the marriage *à
la mode* was, in its own way, a love match, for
upon Sir Vincent's passing, Lady Charlotte had
mourned him very deeply.

Even now, Brandamore noted, there were
faint purple rings beneath her eyes, as if she did
not sleep well at night, and the waiflike quality
that had always characterized her personality
was even more pronounced than usual in her de-
pendence upon her favored cousin. But her mind
was easily distracted, he knew, and it was not
good or proper for a female so young to spend
the rest of her life grieving for a marriage that
had lasted only three years.

"Sally had the nerve to introduce me to someone or another last night as the *dowager* Mrs. Woodville!" Nonetheless incisive for its softness, Lady Charlotte's voice cut neatly through her cousin's reveries. "I *ask* you!"

"No need to enact a Cheltenham Tragedy over it," Brandamore retorted. From an inner pocket, he extracted an ivory snuffbox. With a single gesture that many would-be pinks had long sought to imitate, he flicked back the lid and raised a delicate pinch of his own blend to his nostril. "Since Woodville stuck his spoon in the wall, that's exactly what you are!"

Lady Charlotte's face crumbled slightly. "Dowager! It makes one feel quite like a dowd! And now that I am going back into colors again, I find that all the fashions have changed so much that I shall have to give everything to Elder! I cannot help but feel that Vincent would not have approved of the title *dowager!*"

"Vincent would have been the first one to tell you to make your comeback with panache, and hang the dowager! I hope you're throwin' out that dashed lilac bonnet. With that yellow head of yours, it makes you look paste-faced."

"Paste-faced! George!" Lady Charlotte protested faintly, drawing her white silk shawl up about her shoulders. "Why, Vincent was wont to say that I looked quite fetching in that bonnet!"

"And Vincent, whatever else one may say of him, would have told you you looked ravishing in a gunnysack! No! Out it goes!" Brandamore sneezed, regarding his cousin with a practiced eye. "Tell you what, Charl', go and buy yourself one of those chipstraws, with some plaid ribands. Tell you, plaid will set you up proper this winter, for I intend to bring it into fashion. Been readin' some of those novels of Scott's."

"Plaid?" Lady Charlotte asked dubiously.

"Grandmother was a MacPherson. I've set my tailor to making me a waistcoat in the family tartans. Just for the country, mind you, and just in the family plaids, but don't start babblin' away about it to everyone, Charl', 'til Scott's next novel comes along."

Lady Charlotte never read more than the court circular, so she nodded brightly. "Of course, for day only. Perhaps a shawl—it might look quite amusing for a walk in the park. But what shall I wear for Lady Sefton's ball next week? It will be my first appearance in colors, you know . . ."

Brandamore shrugged. "Blue. Celestial blue silk," he pronounced.

Lady Charlotte sighed, nodding, as Basile entered the room with the sherry tray. "Celestial blue, then, with the Venice silk and bishop sleeves. Do you think slashing would be too daring?"

Basile gave a discreet cough. "The morning mail has arrived, milady. I have taken the liberty of placing yours upon the tray."

"Thank you, Basile," her ladyship responded,

picking up the sheaf of envelopes and idly paging through them. "One good thing, George, no one seems to have forgotten me in my absence. The invitations are coming in! Oh, this one is for Christian." Delicately, she laid aside a long envelope with the seal of an art dealer.

"Christian!" Lord Brandamore snorted at the mention of Lady Charlotte's stepson. "Thank God he ain't about today. Basile told me he was off to an auction at Christie's."

"*Why* you and Christian must always be at odds-heads is beyond me," Lady Charlotte murmured, paging through the invitations.

"Man's a dashed thorn in my side! All Corinthians are," Brandamore said simply. "A bigger lot of slow-tops would be hard to find. 'Sides, Christian makes me uncomfortable."

Her ladyship's lashes fluttered. "Perhaps Christian is a trifle Quakerish at times, but even you must admit that he is of the highest ton! Oh, he will complain about my expenses, of course, but his mama left her entire fortune to him, you know, and he is quite quite warm in his own right, even without what poor Vincent left him. And his taste is as exquisite as yours, you must admit—tho' perhaps a trifle more understated," she added swiftly.

"Man's as dull as dishwater! Why, that waistcoat he was wearin' last night was two months out of style! Oh, he'll complain about your expenses, but when it comes to layin' down his

blunt for some whey-faced painting"—his lordship waved a hand about the Giottos on the
walls— "there's no stoppin' him! I say, dashed if
I'd want a lot of dead people I ain't even related
to staring down at me from every room in my
house."

"Christian is very interested in the arts," Lady
Charlotte agreed. "I could not tell a Rembrandt
from a Holbein, but Vincent was very careful to
have my likeness taken by Romney. As it may
be, Christian and I have always managed to rub
together tolerably well, all things considered, and
it is far better to be his hostess on Upper Mount
Street than to be sent back to Berkshire to live
with Mama and my sisters, which I assure you
would be deadly!"

Lord Brandamore, thinking about his Aunt
Aurelia, one of his less favored relations, silently
agreed to this.

"Besides, George, now that I am a widow, I
shall have ever so much more freedom than I
did as a debutante, and I intend to enjoy it
thoroughly."

"Ha! The devil you say! And what does Christian have to say about that? He's a dashed high
stickler!"

"Christian would, of course, not approve at
all. But, as long as I have his protection and
your favor to rely on, I doubt that London
would have very much to say about anything I
chose to do," Lady Charlotte said naively.

"Well, just be careful you don't end up like Ellen Kimbrough! And if you've heard the latest *on-dit* that Byron fathered that brat of hers, it ain't true!"

Lady Charlotte's eyes opened very wide, and Brandamore swiftly guessed that he had overestimated his cousin's sophistication in the world.

She frowned slightly, considering this. "Well, I don't intend to go that far. But, George, I'm not anxious to hang out for another husband quite yet. Like you, I've decided not to be marriage-minded. No, I think that I quite enjoy my present status—but Christian causes me no end of bother! Season after season, I have trotted out the most eligible belles for his inspection, and that dreadful man will simply not choose a one of them! It seems to me that the best thing that could happen to him would be a wife and several children—" She broke off, looking curiously down at the handwriting on one epistle. "Well, of all things famous!"

"Whatzzat?" Brandamore stirred imperceptibly from his customary lethargy.

"A letter of all things! Who do we know who actually writes letters? Everyone is in town for the season, after all." Lady Charlotte inserted a nail beneath the seal and spread the neatly folded sheet, holding it quite close to her face, for those fabled blue eyes were lent a great deal of their misty beauty by her nearsightedness.

Fluff, the little dog Brandamore had unceremoniously dumped upon the carpet, stole up to his lordship and rubbed against his boot, and his lordship absently stroked him, quite forgetting that one of his major pets was small, furry lapdogs. Absently, he raised his quizzing glass and surveyed the walls of the green salon. Little as he liked to admit anything good about Christian Woodville, the man did have excellent taste in paintings. His collection of Renaissance masters had to be one of the best in Europe—too bad that the man was such a dashed slow-top! Of course, Lord Brandamore's vanity would never allow him to admit that he disliked Woodville most of all for being one of the few members of the ton who ignored his own strictures upon fashion and did exactly as he pleased without losing as much as a speck of his own desirability as one of the bucks of the town.

"Of all things!" Lady Charlotte repeated. "George, d'you recall Elise Pellerin?"

"Pellerin? Ain't they Distanning's brood from Devon?"

"Of course not, goose! Her people are—*were,* I should say—*aristos.* Quite a dreadful story, I believe. The family was simply *filthy* with titles and honors—they barely escaped from the Terror alive. Well, poor Elise and her brother and their uncle Comte Auguste Pellerin escaped. Her parents and the rest of the family were all guillotined!" Lady Charlotte shuddered delicately and pressed one hand against her own fragile throat.

Brandamore examined his well-manicured fingernails. "Bit of a bad show, what? Of course, you could never trust the Froggies. Thank God that sort of thing can't happen here in England, I say! So, what of another *émigré* family?"

"Well, I was at Miss Copplestone's Seminary in Bath with Elise—"

Brandamore raised one eyebrow in his famous gesture. "Sendin' you to school with an *émigré?* I say, did Aunt Aurelia know?"

Lady Charlotte carelessly brushed the laces off her lap and tossed aside *The Lady's Journal.* "Of course, Elise and I became bosom-brows, you know. She was very good at helping me with my French. Her uncle managed to cut some paintings out of their frames and smuggle them away, and when he came to England, he set himself up as an art dealer—I believe that Christian knows him somehow— Oh, I assure you, it was the most courageous thing, for none of them had the faintest idea of how to go on, any more than you or I would if we had lost everything and been forced to take up a trade in a strange country; but Comte Auguste did amazingly well, you see, and he was determined that Elise and Noel should have the best English education."

"Still and all, dashed bad ton, I say, settin' up with a pack of *émigrés.*" Brandamore yawned. "Not our sort of people at all."

"Oh, be quiet, do!" Lady Charlotte said

firmly. "They are quite respectable, I assure you. Comte Pellerin owns one of the most prestigious and respected galleries in the city, and he has made *pots* of money, to boot! The thing is, since Elsie has come down from Miss Copplestone's, she has been living with her brother near Oxford, where he has been studying. I imagine she's been keeping house for him. Poor dear! It must be as dull as dishwater with nothing but schoolboys and dons! Poor, dear Elise, buried in that country town, with nothing to do. Why, she does not even mention a beau! No proper come-out, no Almack's, nothing to do all day, I suppose, but that painting and sketching of hers. I recall that her watercolors were quite above the ordinary sort of thing we all turned out, but really—" Lady Charlotte sighed, "here she is all of one and twenty and still not married! Why, she's practically an ape-leader!"

"Sounds like a regular country mouse," Brandamore yawned.

"Ah, but, George, the most famous thing! Her brother Noel has come down from university, and the comte wishes them both to remove to London so that Noel may take up an occupation. How very nice it will be to see Elise again!"

"See her?" Lord Brandamore exclaimed. "Surely you, Charl', ain't goin' to renew acquaintance with an *émigré* who smells of the shop!"

"George, do not, I ask of you, be an insuffer-able bore," Lady Charlotte commanded. "Deal-ing with works of art can hardly constitute smelling of the shop! That's not *trade*— Why, Lord Duveen and Petersham both buy and sell art."

Brandamore shrugged. "Well, you do have to admit, Charl', that aside from Madame de Staël and Talleyrand, damned few of these Frenchies are tonnish!"

"Which means, no doubt," Lady Charlotte said thoughtfully, "that poor Elise will spend her time in London with a deadly dull set of old *aris-tos,* all mourning for the old days at Versailles? Why, when Elise left France, she was barely old enough to know what was going on, let alone re-call Marie Antoinette. It is a great deal too bad! When I recall how Elise would always help me with my French, and how she could always coax Cook into smuggling us an extra cherry tart, and how clever she was about smuggling a *billet* from the madly handsome half-pay officer to me past Miss Copplestone— Oh, I must see her! She was always the handsomest creature, too—very dark, and very tall. People used to call us the sun and the moon, you know . . ."

Lord Brandamore's yawn was politely stifled by the unexpected entrance of a tall gentleman. While the gentleman's shirt points were not so high as to make the turning of his head an impossibility, and only one plain fob dangled from the gold watch chain on his gray waistcoat, his coat proclaimed the artistry of Scott, and his pale buckskins needed no padding to fill out the lines of his calves. "I say, Charlotte, you should have—" he began without preamble; then catching sight of Brandamore, he frowned. "Oh, it's *you*," he said flatly. With his long, careless stride, he made his way across the room and poured himself a glass of sherry, then leaned against the marble mantelpiece, obviously in no hurry to depart. "Teasin' Charlotte with the latest fashionable fribble, George?" he demanded.

Brandamore raised his quizzing glass and leveled a cold stare at Mr. Woodville. The sight of Brandamore's hideously magnified eye had been known to throw lesser men than Woodville into strong confusion, but Christian merely rolled his eyes and sipped at his sherry, informing his absurdly young stepmother that he had sold two Flemish watercolors and dropped in upon Turner's studio for a chat.

The sight of Christian Woodville had never failed to stir the faintest tinge of jealousy in Brandamore's heart of hearts. His figure was tall and well made, the result of a vigorous pursuit of the sporting life. His raven locks had no need of the pomades and powders employed by those gentlemen of less fortunate appearance. A leveler that had slipped under his guard in Jackson's Boxing Saloon had given his ancestral nose a certain slightly bent cast which in no way diminished the attraction of his rugged countenance; and a pair of ice gray eyes, fringed with dark lashes that might have been the envy of many a belle, instead had the power to cause those same ladies a feeling of attraction toward their owner to which, at seven and twenty, he seemed entirely indifferent. His broad mouth was of a firm set, and when he delivered one of his infrequent smiles, he tended to lift only one corner of his mouth in a twisted grin that his best friends described as devilish.

Defeated again, Brandamore allowed his glass to depend upon its riband. "I was just tellin' Charl' that waistcoat you was wearin' last night at the opera was at least two months out of fashion! Silver buttons, my boy, are the crack and the go these days! Scott's a dead bore, old man, Ought to see my tailor, Nugie, instead!"

This shaft fell far of its mark, for Woodville merely shrugged his shoulders. Today his waistcoat was of a pale beige basket-shade, and his coat a chocolate superfine. The points of his neck cloth were not, as Lord Brandamore's, so high that he could not turn his head either to the right or the left, and his neck cloth was arranged with negligent neatness. His boots were glossy, but not ornamented with the gold tassels Lord

Brandamore decreed currently fashionable, and
his buckskin breeches, while cut to show that his
legs were in no need of padding, were not too
tight that he must feel some trepidation in
seating himself. A single gold seal dangled from
his watch chain, and he wore a black mourning
band upon his arm. In short, Mr. Woodville's
attire was in every way a contrast to Lord Brandamore's sartorial splendor.

Lady Charlotte, sensing yet another contre-
temps brewing, quickly interposed. "George was
just telling me the last crim con, Christian! Did
you know that Byron is said to have—"

Woodville drained off his sherry, shaking his
head slightly. "Heard it. Actually, Charlotte,
that's what I've come to speak to you about.
Now that we're going back into colors, well, *we*
are upon the verge of being the latest *on-dit!*"

Lady Charlotte blinked. "You and I? But
how?"

Woodville sighed. There were times when
Charlotte's obtuseness sorely tried his affectionate patience for his late father's wife. Fond as
he was of her, he could not help but feel that the
old man had spoiled and sheltered her far beyond what should have been necessary for the
very young wife of an older man cast adrift in
the treacherous waters of London society. "A
very young wife and a stepson only a few years
her senior livin' under the same roof is inevitably
bound to cause *some* comment. When m'father

was here, it was different, of course, and if there had been, well, a child, it might have rectified matters—" He was trying his best to be gentle, but Brandamore started.

"What, you an' Charl' doin' the indecent! Not by half, I'll be bound! You ain't at all in her style!"

"No, I do not think that Christian and I should suit at all, as anyone knows! Why, it would be like" —her hands fluttered delicately— "it would be like—with one's own brother, really!"

Christian thrust his hands deep into his pockets, a gesture that never failed to irritate Brandamore. "I'm not sayin' that I want to get rid of you, Charlotte—put you off in the dower house at Woodville, or any such thing. For one thing, m'father stipulated that you was to have the use of this house until you remarried, or I married, which ain't likely, by half; but I don't like the way people talk any more than you do—and talk they will. I've been thinkin' that it might be a good idea if my Aunt Lavinia were to come down from Bath—"

"No!" Charlotte implored. All of her late husband's relations had not taken to the marriage as well as his son, and Lavinia, a dragonish spinster of stern religious principles, least of all. "She would eat me alive, Christian, you know she would! Why, it would always be a come-down about my clothes, or my conduct, or any number of things. She would be far more disapproving than you ever could be! And you know how you can cut up stiff over the merest trifles!"

Since Mr. Woodville had been forced to rescue his stepmother from the folly of her own naïveté several times since his father's death, and since he was not the most patient of men when involved with the female sex, he was forced to acknowledge the truth of this statement. "But that's why you need another female about, Charlotte! It would be a dashed thing if you was to fall into the rogue-points! M'father asked me to make sure that you were taken care of after he blew his spoon; but Charlotte, there are so many times when our engagements and friends differ that I can't always be there! Fond of you, Charlotte, but for that very reason, I feel we need some sort of a duenna to give countenance to our situation here! Aunt Lavinia's the only female I can think of."

"But I have Brandamore—" Lady Charlotte protested.

"All the more reason to have a duenna! Between the two of you, you've already managed to set London on its heels, and there's more than one old tartar who'd love to see your reputation in shreds. As well as my own," he added absently, pulling out his watch. In a more gentle tone, he continued, "Think upon it, Charlotte.

Even this fop will admit that there's sense in what I say. You may whoop and carry on all about London, if you wish, but without the protection of a husband, a young and very pretty widow is fair game for every wagging tongue at Almack's. I've got to be pushing off, now. I'm due at my club."

With a bow toward Lady Charlotte and a laconic nod of his head toward Brandamore, Mr. Woodville closed the doors behind him.

There was a moment of silence. As she began to comprehend what Christian had said, Lady Charlotte's face took on a look of extreme distress. "Just when I am about to go out and enjoy meself—Aunt Lavinia! She quite terrifies me! Oh, if Vincent were here, this would not have happened! How excessively vexing of him to take a chill like that, and leave me all alone!" She looked very much as if she were about to indulge in one of her increasingly less-frequent bouts of weeping for her late husband.

"There, now, there!" Brandamore exclaimed uncomfortably, going as far as to extricate himself from his chair and taking her hand. "Damned cold fish, Christian! Always was! But you must admit that there is truth in what he says. Odd situation—young son, young widow under the same roof—bound to give rise to talk. And I doubt that even my influence would be able to stop the gossips," he added pompously.

"As if I were a Messalina!" Lady Charlotte sniffed. She pressed a hand against her bosom. "As if there were any man I could possibly form a tender for but my dear, dear Vincent—"

"There, there," Brandamore said soothingly. Even Miss Woodville can't quite prevent you from entertaining or going out—"

"But she will sniff, and tiptoe about, and the servants can't stand her, and she will positively cast gloom everywhere! Missionary meetings!" Lady Charlotte added darkly. "I should rather go home to Mama!"

As she searched for her handkerchief amidst the pile of laces on the sofa, her hand brushed Miss Pellerin's letter. She was about to toss it aside when a rare flash of insight glimmered inside her mind, inspired, perhaps, by an instinct for self-preservation.

"Elise!" she exclaimed, the clouds clearing away from her face.

"Pardon?" Brandamore asked, understandably startled.

"Elise Pellerin! Of course! Why did I not think of it immediately! Why, she is a thousand times, no, a million times better than Aunt Aurelia! Why, she always looked after me at school—the half pay officer was, of course, totally ineligible, or I never would have found my dear Vincent, you know, billeted in some garrison town; but Elise should have her chance, and I should have my duenna, and Christian will be satisfied, and that shall stop odious people like that dreadful Drummond-Burrel creature from talking. Sally, of course, would issue her a voucher, and you can bring her into fashion, George! There! Vincent always said that if I would *only* contrive to develop my thoughts a bit faster, I would be right as trivet! Elise! She would be perfect—if, of course, the comte will allow her to stay here. But how could he refuse, when she has devoted the past four years to a very dull life for her brother? I'm sure it will be just the thing! And perhaps I might even contrive to find her a husband of some sort!"

"Charl'," Lord Brandamore said uneasily, but Lady Charlotte turned a radiant face toward him and slipped her hand inside of his own.

"Only think how amusing it would be, George, to launch not only a total unknown, but an *émigré* into the ton! Why, between you and me, we could have all of London at her feet! Only think what a delight it would be to watch them all scrambling to her feet, all because we have declared her to be an Incomparable! And that way, you see, I should have a duenna, and a perfectly marvelous way to reenter society! I have never presented anyone before, you know; I daresay it would be good practice; and Elise is ever so much better than Aunt Aurelia; and it would repay her for all of the things she did for me at school!"

"An *émigré?*" Brandamore asked dubiously, his face turning a delicate pale. "An unknown, penniless *émigré?* Really, Charl', you would always have your sister Louisa launched this year—"

"And that would mean Mama, which is as bad as Aunt Aurelia. Besides, Mama means to keep her back another year, in hopes that her spots will clear up. No, I tell you, Elise is perfect!"

Brandamore chewed his mustaches thoughtfully. "Well, I can't quite see—I mean, not our sort of people, after all—"

Lady Charlotte thrust out her lower lip. "George St. Ives! You are forever saying that with your power you could launch a scullery maid who weighed eighteen stone into the heights of the ton! And you won't even bestir yourself in the slightest for a perfectly charming female with the most tragic history, not even for me? Would you prefer to have Aunt Aurelia sitting over there with her terrible tracts, sniffing and muttering about sin every time you and I plan as much as a rout party?"

Lord Brandamore straightened his shoulders. A faint gleam had entered his dark eyes, and the faintest smile played about his lips. Delicately, he touched one shirt point, and fondled the carnation in his buttonhole. "It would be a bit of a lark, don't you know, watching them all vying to make her a Diamond of the First Water—the toast of the town, and a good marriage by the end of Michaelmas! By Gad, Charl', it just might be the thing to enliven a dull season!"

Lady Charlotte, feeling a resurgence of her old Olympian power, nodded. "Why, it's almost as if we're fairy godparents! I shall have a chaperone, and Elise shall see a bit of society, and, if we are clever, find a very good husband—of course, it would be of all things wonderful, but not entirely necessary, if she had a title— Why, she shall be just like Cinderella! And Christian cannot possibly object!"

Lord Brandamore was moved by his own vision. "So damned novel, don't you know, to be doing something good, instead of ripping someone's character to shreds! Wonderful! Come, my dear, and ring old Basile for another bottle of sherry. We must compose a letter immediately. I do hope the old man don't kick up stiff!"

"But, of course," Lady Charlotte said, laughing sunnily. "I shall immediately compose a note to the comte, and of course, I must consult Elder, for Elise will no doubt need a new wardrobe— Oh, it will be so much fun shopping together again—Madame Celeste, of course— and a ball, not only to mark our emergence from mourning, but also to introduce my new companion and friend into our world! And, of course, by the time we have her married off, it will be time to launch Louisa; so I daresay I may put Aunt Lavinia off for at least five years—one for each sister!"

And the two cousins put their fair heads together, planning as they had in days of old.

Chapter Two

"There! Yvonne, that is the last of the dishes!" Miss Elise Pellerin straightened up, standing back to inspect the neatly bound wicker chest. She wiped her hands on the gray apron bound about her ancient green and white striped merino gown, and pushed the limp mobcap further back over her russetish curls, leaving a long streak of dust across her forehead.

"That I should see the day!" The portly maid-servant to whom this remark was addressed pushed her sleeves farther up her sturdy arms, looking sadly at the girl who had been in her charge since birth. In her opinion, *la princesse* had no right to be packing dishes in the kitchen of an insignificant townhouse on Little Clarendon Crescent. For, within Yvonne's memory of the old days, *la princesse* would never have seen the inside of a kitchen, let alone soil her hands in the matter of removing household. That Elise had been barely toddling then did not matter.

Nonetheless, Yvonne murmured beneath her breath and employed a clean corner of her own apron to wipe away the smudge on her charge's forehead.

"*En anglais,* Yvonne, *toujours en anglais.* Remember that we no longer speak French," Elise said softly with a glance at the burly carter's lads who were moving the cartons into the wagon outside the door.

Yvonne sniffed, giving her skirts a kick. "*Les cochons anglais,* always with their suspicions. Do we return to France for this Bonaparte? Do we send him English secrets from this little town of students and professors? Bah! I shake the dust of this dull place off my skirts with pleasure! *Le comte,* he should have sent for you long ago to come to London, and found you a proper husband, instead of burying you here *avec votre frère, le prince!*"

Elise patted her old nurse's arm comfortingly. "I have been happy here, happier, I think, than I should be in London. I shall miss this house, and the garden and the boating, and all our friends." She looked about the sadly empty kitchen. "It is a great deal too bad that I cannot stay on here alone, for I know that I shall never have the light at Auguste's quite as well as I have had it here—" She looked up toward the ceiling, as if she could see through the floors to the third story where, until yesterday, she had kept her painting studio set up just as she liked it, away from the prying eyes of all but a few friends. Then she shrugged her shoulders, one of her few vestigial Gallic gestures. "But in London, Yvonne, we shall have the museums and the galleries and visits from our friends! How very nice it will be to see Mr. Turner's studio!" A sly grin flickered across her face. "And Auguste will finally give me a show all of my own! Just think of that! Twenty canvases he will frame and exhibit in his gallery!"

Yvonne nodded, glad that her charge was taking well their remove to the metropolis. Of the two children she had brought over from France to these unknown shores, risking her own life in the ordeal, Noel would always, of course, be her baby, to be fussed and clucked over. Elise, two years older than her brother, had always been more independent, the practical one. Both of them were good-looking young people; they had inherited their Italian mother's dark, even complexion, and their French father's fine, chiseled bone-structure. The young female who stood next to her would be considered handsome rather than beautiful by the milk and rosewater English standards: her eyes were too dark and too intelligent, her nose, aquiline rather than the fashionable retrousse, her lips, while quite rosy, perhaps too wide, and her chin was set at a determined angle; and her figure perhaps a shade too tall and too voluptuous in a time when the rage was all for dainty sylphs, but, eh, Yvonne thought, a man would have to be deaf, blind and half-dead not to appreciate the graceful curve of her neck, or the self-assured elegance of her carriage. Even an ancient dress which Yvonne had twice deposited in the dustbin and twice seen removed by her charge to be laundered and worn again and again could not quite disguise the fact that here was the daughter of excellent blood. No matter that her late, blessed mother's jewels would never adorn her, or that she would never stroll, as had her father, through the palace at Versailles in brocades and silks. No matter that the vast estates in Lorraine which would have formed her *dot* were no longer hers; in the not uncritical eyes of her preceptress, the lady who chose to be called simply Miss Elise Pellerin was still every inch *la princesse* Elizabet-Marie Theresa Pellerin d'Angelle!

Yvonne sniffed again, absently turning the cuffs of the disreputable merino dress. It was not, to her mind, inconceivable that Elise had been, from time to time, the object of veneration of several young gentlemen, nor that she had gently but firmly turned down at least two offers for her hand. One of these swains had been the stout son of a country baronet from Hampshire, and the other a rather romantic-notioned young lordling of fine connections to royalty. But in Yvonne's mind, neither would have ever been peer to Elise's exalted rank. Had she known that Miss Pellerin had begged away, not from a sense of inferior alliance, but from a very real sense that such a marriage would have put an end to the entire *raison d'être* of her being, she would, not unnaturally, have been quite shocked.

All young ladies received some instruction in sketching and watercolors as a good and necessary part of their finishing. Most of them were quite untalented, merely amusing themselves with pencil and brush in much the same way they had once played with mud pies, biding their time until the right gentlemen should occupy their time with the duties of matrimony. Unfortunately, Miss Pellerin's talents had been something quite above the ordinary. Nurtured by a fond uncle whose life and career were devoted to the cultivation and appreciation of artists, and placed in the hands of an excellent educator in the form of Miss Copplestone, Elise's skills had developed and flourished far beyond what might have been expected. Angelica Kauffmann herself had been her instructor for several years, and she had also had the shrewd critiques of Maria Cosway. Visiting her uncle in the metropolis had allowed her to observe, without being observed, the movements of the art world. A handful of artists were aware of her work, and their en-

couragement was sufficient for her to entertain
certain rather modest ambitions for her own
painting.

"She paints like a man!" Christian Woodville
had exclaimed upon viewing a small landscape
of the Oxfordshire countryside, and while that
noted critic may have directed the remark as
praise of Elise's talents, she had suddenly understood something very important. First, that she
was possessed of the very natural desire of any
creative person to receive recognition for her
efforts, a most heady and gratifying experience; and secondly, that females, even Miss
Kauffmann and Mrs. Cosway, no matter how tal-
ented or innovative their efforts, never achieved
the status of their male counterparts.

Even her uncle, who appreciated her works
enough to grant her a small exhibition in one of
his lesser rooms, had admitted that had she been
a male, her success would have been far greater.
The simple fact was clear to her: As artists,
women were simply not held in the same esteem
as men. But the delicate portraits of blushing
madonnas and fragile still-life canvases to which
custom seemed to limit her sex, when, indeed, it
chose to accept them at all, were not for Elise. In
her secret heart, her ambitions were far higher,
and to achieve this end, she had conceived what
she considered a most satisfactory plan.

In part, her lack of reluctance to leave the
peace of Oxford was tempered by this secret.

Certainly, it would make the transition to city life far more easy for her to accept, and even to look forward to.

And, of course, there was Noel. . . .

Noel had always come first, and now that he had come down from university and must find some respectable career suitable to his situation in life, it was more than ever important that they remove to the city. Unfortunately, no one had yet decided what a handsome young man with a great deal of charm and not a whit of ambition beyond acquiring a bit of town bronze could do; but like her uncle and Yvonne, Elise was fond enough of her treasured younger brother to hope that he might attain some quite respectable and well-paid post which would elevate him toward self-support in the style to which his uncle's fortune had accustomed him.

Yvonne, finished with her ministrations to Miss Pellerin's toilette, clucked her tongue. "Your brother pays too much attention to his clothes, and you not enough!" she admonished her charge. "And, where, I would like to know, is that *jeune homme?* He should have been home hours ago to see that his wardrobe was packed!"

"I daresay he's out saying goodbye to his friends," Elise murmured absently, watching as several of her heavily wrapped canvases were carried past her and out the doorway.

"I hope he is not with M'sieu Emile, gambling! That one is no good! M'sieu Bertraine, with all his airs and graces—if his sainted parents could see how he had turned his hand, *alors,* how ashamed they would be, a Bertraine turning his hand to *la fortune!*" Yvonne frowned disapprovingly, the corners of her lips drawn almost down to her plump chin. "You! Do not treat that chair like a sack of grain!" The burly individual to whom this invective was directed looked as if he were sorely tempted to drop the furniture in question then and there, along with his notice, and Elise gently propelled her mentor out of the line of the workmen, through the empty rooms of the small house that had been their home for so long.

"I do hope Mr. Crinchley will find tenants who will love this place as much as I have," Elise sighed, leading Yvonne up the stairs to her brother's room. Together, they began to remove his shirts from the clothespress, folding them away into the carelessly packed trunks Noel had abandoned. "Really, Yvonne, you should not be so hard on poor M'sieu Emile! After all, his lot has been no less pleasant than ours, and it would be a terrible thing for us to turn our backs upon a fellow *émigré,* especially a man whom we have known for all our lives! Even Uncle Auguste admits that Emile has a certain talent for gambling—and each one of us had best turn his hand to that which suits him to survive! The Chevalier Blanchette is a shoremaker now, and Comtesse de Gury is known not for her head-dresses, but her sweet ices! Is it not enough that we have survived the Terror! We should all be thankful that we may turn our hands to some work!"

"Bah!" Yvonne countered, lovingly removing a corbeau coat from the press and spreading it in tissue. "Honest work I do not object much to make! But Emile, he is—what you say—a Captain Sharp! If Noel follows his ways, he will bring ruin upon us all!"

Elise frowned. She knew that there was truth in what Yvonne said—Emile Bertraine was not the sort of person one would have encouraged, under ordinary circumstances, to run tame in their household. But he was a fellow *émigré,* and those bonds of loyalty which wound their invisible threads through the network of French exiles living in England could not be so easily cast aside. And besides, it was so hard to doubt seriously the intentions of a man one had known since cradle days, whose parents had perished upon the same guillotine as one's own.

"Here, now, what's all this about Emile?" a sulky voice demanded, and the two women turned to behold a darkly handsome youth lounging in the doorway, his dark brows drawn down over his large brown eyes, his mouth petulant, as he surveyed his sister and his old nurse.

The chance observer could not fail to remark upon the resemblance between the Pellerins, brother and sister. But where Elise might have been considered tolerably attractive, if perhaps a bit of an Original, Noel had been blessed with an almost breathtaking handsomeness. From the abundance of russet-black curls which adorned his even-featured face to the ten toes of his well-formed feet, Noel Pellerin had been from birth one of those rare human beings blessed with perfection. The darling of an older sister, the perpetual *enfant* of an indulgent nurse, and the shining hope of an aristocratic uncle, he had grown into his young manhood firmly convinced of his own worth in the world. Far more than his sister, he had accepted the dictates of his nurse and uncle that he was of the bluest blood in the *ancien régime,* and he had never ceased to regret the tides of history which had swept away his rightful place in the world, even though he had been spirited away from that world when not much more than an infant in swaddling clothes. That he must make his way in the world by his own labor was a fact that he would much rather have ignored, for as a schoolboy and the student, he had been more than generously endowed by his uncle's funds to indulge in every fond thing which might take his fancy.

"Noel!" Elise said in the tone closest to a scold she could ever manage for her brother. "You were supposed to be home hours ago, and packing your clothes! Uncle's chaise will be here by teatime, and Yvonne and I have yet to bathe and change!"

But Noel, unimpressed by these strictures, merely yawned, stretching his arms high above his head to reveal a particularly bright waistcoat of cherry striped silk with silver buttons. "Sorry, I'm sure! But I was out all of last night—a group of us went to the Mermaid for one last go-about, and there was a bit of a scrape about a bear" — he yawned again, exposing two rows of perfect white teeth— "that we put into the bagwig's rooms, into his bed as a matter of fact, which I bet Charlie Cecil we could not do; so will you give me a fiver, Elise? Got to make good on my debts, y'know!"

Elise, deciding that she wanted to hear nothing about bears and bagwigs, shook her head. "When you've packed your things, I'll give you a note, and you may have it sent round to Charles' rooms. Noel, out all night, and not a wink of sleep, you'll be so tired by the time we get to London that you'll take sick again!"

"Eh bien, mon petit," Yvonne worried, inspecting her charge for signs of damage. "How do you expect your uncle to attain a good position for you with someone like Mr. Woodville, when you will be dead from such rough living before you even leave Oxford? Out all night, no doubt with Emile Bertraine, *et ces viagères, ces femmes-de-vie—*"

"Oh, Yvonne, *ma vieille,* do leave off!" Noel laughed. "Emile's in London or Newmarket, and

I swear to you it was just the lads last night, kicking up a lark—"

Elise shook her head and slipped quietly out of the room.

"Anyway, it's about time Uncle Auguste gave me a man of my own, a valet, instead of my nanny fussing all about me—"

Their voices, in the ancient litany, followed her up the steps to her studio.

The room was really little more than a garret. In the cold light, stripped of all her dear and familiar objects, it looked sad and barren indeed. Dark squares on the walls betrayed the places where she had hung her paintings, and smudges of paint and oilseed on the floor gave testimony to the hard, and not always completely neat, way in which she worked.

Picking up the skirts of her gown from the dusty floor, Elise moodily crossed the empty room and stared out the window at the autumnal remains of the garden. For her, the room suddenly seemed to be filled with ghostly impressions—hours of work, small gatherings of friends laughing and discussing art and literature around the oil stove. A quiet, simple, well-ordered life.

And now, all that was about to end. Oh, there would be a space made for her at her uncle's house on Half Moon Street, and she would preside over his dinner parties and dutifully entertain what members of the *ancien régime* could still come to call, their Parisian French endlessly, endlessly picking over and over again the days of Versailles, Louis and Marie—days she had no memory of, a time as distant and removed from her as if it had all been conducted on the other side of the moon. She might even be asked for her opinion on this or that painter or sculptor as she begged Romney to help himself to a bit more of the asparagus points or poured tea for Phillips. Just for one fleeting second she thought longingly of her friend Charlotte St. Ives—what a life she must lead, with gay parties and balls and not a thought in her head but which invitation to answer, or which dress to wear for a drive in the park.

But Charlotte would never know the fulfillment of standing back from a hard-fought bit of work no larger than her fingernail on a canvas, or understand the particular pleasure of observing a particularly beautiful Leonardo.

But still, sometimes, one could wish that there was just a little more, a person, perhaps, to whom one could turn to share that little piece of painting, or the pleasure of Leonardo.

She shook the thought out of her head. If ever she had cherished secret hopes of someday encountering precisely that sort of a gentleman, she had folded them away like an old sketching book.

No. There were other plans to be made.

For the hundredth time, she considered what she would say to persuade her uncle that while a female artist under the name of Miss Pellerin might be lightly shrugged off as a charming dilettante, an unknown and obsessively reclusive painter who signed works with the *nom-de-peinture* E. M. d'Angelle would certainly cause the world to stand up and take note!

She wrapped her arms tightly about herself, wondering why Mr. Woodville had found it necessary to compliment her by saying she painted like a man. No matter. In fact, she was certainly in his debt, for that chance remark, uttered so carelessly during her last visit to London, had inspired the scheme she ardently hoped would make her fortune.

Chapter Three

Seated behind his enormous desk of teak and inlaid ebony, Auguste, Comte Pellerin, presented the world with the perfect portrait of a man who has managed to straddle two very different worlds. Even in repose, he retained both the image of an aristocrat, for he had never quite lost the courtly manner acquired in the youth spent at Versailles, and that other, more mundane aspect of the man of the business world, into which necessity had forced him, and fate had kindly allowed him to prosper.

Eighteen years ago, he had arrived upon English soil with a rudimentary understanding of the native tongue and the raw memory of almost the whole of his ancient and distinguished lineage's being erased in a single day, almost every trace of his comfortable world vanished in the blood of the Terror. A lesser man might have broken beneath the strain and the loss, but M. le Comte, with the charge of a small nephew and niece and one faithful retainer, had immediately recognized that his duty lay in providing for his charges. For four people brought up from birth to receive every material comfort as their due, the first two years of poverty and alienation in a strange country had been hard times indeed. But like many of his fellows, M. le Comte had used his Gallic practicality and shrewdness to turn a pastime into a living, and a lifelong passion for the fine arts had reaped him handsome dividends in a country prosperous with a wartime economy and an industrial upheaval in which many a self-made man wished to shake the dust of the factory from his heels by acquiring such trappings of the "good life" as high art.

M. le Comte's tastes were excellent, and his knowledge of painting encyclopedic. It was not long before his elegant establishment on Bond Street enjoyed the patronage of the very highest ton as well as the warmest cits. Within the exalted spheres of the Museum and the Academy, his name carried a great weight, and his purse had grown correspondingly heavier with each passing year.

Fortunately, Auguste's temperament was as sanguine as it was shrewd, and while he would never dream of seeking entry into the ton for himself, he was able to claim acquaintance and frequently intimacy with such members of that set as chose to take an interest in the arts. When M. le Comte entertained, his interests lay as much with feeding the hopeful artists under his patronage as with impressing potential buyers of their art. Being more interested in the quality than the Quality of his company had earned him the reputation for some of the most interesting gatherings in London. One might meet almost anyone else at Comte Pellerin's, it was said, and if the truth were to be told, his entertainments were of more interest than those given by the most exclusive hostesses.

But M. le Comte's thoughts were not upon entertainment that afternoon. Anticipating the arrival of his niece and nephew at his house in Half Moon Street, he was giving desultory attention to a set of miniature landscapes attributed to Benjamin West when his clerk entered the office.

This menial, who was in the habit of addressing himself to a portrait of the late French queen hanging directly above his employer's chair, murmured that Lady Woodville requested audience with his employer.

"Eh? Woodville? Woodville?" M. le Comte exclaimed, laying aside the velvet portfolio case and gesturing the man out with both hands, "Show him in at once, Jean-Claude! You should know better than to keep Woodville waiting! *Vite! Vite!*"

Jean-Claude, whose English was at best indifferent, merely shrugged his way out of the room again.

But when he ushered in Lady Charlotte, very fetchingly attired in a carriage costume consisting of an ivory muslin gown, neatly covered with a pelisse of royal blue velvet, sumptuously trimmed in ermine with matching muff and tippet, a poke bonnet of *rose doré* placed upon her pale curls, and the small Fluff cradled in the crook of her arm, Monsieur's welcoming remarks died away upon his lips.

"Can it be—? but, yes!" he exclaimed as Charlotte lifted her veil, "It is little Charlotte St. Ives, all grown up now! But of course, you are Mrs. Woodville—my condolences, Lady Charlotte! *Alors*, it has been a very long time!"

Hastily, he signaled Jean-Claude to draw up a chair for her ladyship. After ascertaining that she required not so much as a drop of tea to revive herself from the harrowing experience of a ten-minute ride in a barouche all the way from Upper Mount Street to Bond Street, that her mother, the dowager countess, was in good health in Hampshire, that she had just emerged from her mourning for her late husband, a fine man, that Christian Woodville was in good states and very busy with his duties at the Foreign Office, he tactfully awaited enlightenment upon what had brought her to his gallery.

"I had a letter from Elise," Lady Charlotte begun in her soft voice, one small, gloved hand stroking Fluff's silky fur, "and she informs me that Noel is down from Oxford and they are removing to London."

M. le Comte smiled. "Ah, yes! I have high hopes for Noel—I have spoken to Mr. Woodville had to others about the possibility of procuring him a post in the Foreign Office. My nephew, he is very quick. We are very proud of him!" He leaned forward and winked. "He is completely the young English gentleman! Most necessary for a young man to advance in the world. And when I go on, he will have a small trust—"

Lady Charlotte batted her lashes. "Oh, M'sieu Auguste, it will be many years before you pass on! Why, you look as young as you did when we left Miss Copplestone's! And I, I look like a sad dowd—imagine! I am a dowager now!"

Since M. le Comte owed his youthful appearance to the wearing of corsets and the careful ministrations of hair dye by his valet, he allowed himself to preen for a second before placing a fatherly hand upon one of Lady Charlotte's smaller ones. "Nonsense, *ma petite* Charlotte! You are still a schoolgirl, while I, alas, am rapidly approaching my sixieth summer!"

This exchange served to put each so much in

charity with the other that it was quite some time before Lady Charlotte recalled herself to the purpose of her mission. Regretting that the manners of gentlemen in modern times were so lacking in the charm of those of the Court of Versailles, she gave a regretful sigh.

"I suppose that you have given some thought to Elise's entertainment in London, M'sieu Auguste?"

The comte frowned. "Elise? She will, of course, live in my household, and she will have her little painting studio, and, I daresay, she will be happy enough. She is—how do you say?—as good as gold, that one. As long as she can paint, she is happy. I know that she did not wish to leave Oxford, but she has always enjoyed her visits to London, and I suppose she will contrive her own amusements."

Lady Charlotte stroked her dog thoughtfully. Her large blue eyes met M. le Comte's shrewd brown orbs. "M'sieu Auguste, we have known one another since Elise and I were at Miss Copplestone's, have we not?"

"Ah, *oui,* it seems as if it were only yesterday that you and Elise were little girls with *mousse au chocolat* all over your faces. . . ." He sighed.

Lady Charlotte nodded. "And though we are more or less of an age, M'sieu Auguste, I am already a widow, and Elise has no husband at all."

M. le Comte, perhaps sensing what was in the wind, regarded Lady Charlotte from beneath his eyelids. "Elise has never complained. She has never seemed to care . . . for the social life. Noel, now," he added in somewhat heartier tones, but Lady Charlotte immediately cut him off.

"—perhaps because she has never had the chance, M'sieu Auguste! When we came down from school, you, sir, whisked her immediately away to Oxford to look after her brother. And perhaps because she did not know any better, she did enjoy it. But now, M'sieu Auguste, I am a widow, living with my stepson, and I am in a position to place my dear Elise in the forefront of society! You know, of course, that my cousin Lord Brandamore is among the leaders of the ton?"

"As are you, yourself, Lady Charlotte," Auguste agreed. "But Elise—"

"It don't fadge!" Lady Charlotte said firmly. "You see, M'sieu Auguste, my stepson—how very droll it is to have a stepson seven years one's senior!—feels that I should have a female companion now that I am to go back into society again. He feels that because he and I are so much of an age, people will talk. People really seem to do very little else in our set. I know, because I talk all the time," she added naively.

"But Elsie is an *émigré*," M. le Comte pointed out reasonably. *"Les aristos anglais, ils n'aiment pas les aristos d'ancien régime français,"* he pointed out. "If you mean to bring my niece out in society, I fear that you will only cause her to be hurt by snubs and slights. Believe me, I know that of which I speak!"

Lady Charlotte shook her head. "Well, it won't fadge," she repeated. "Because Brandamore can do anything he choses to do, and I have a great deal of cachet! Indeed, I am considered to be all the crack!" This last immodest pronouncement did more to betray her innocence than anything else she could have said.

A smile played about M. le Comte's lips. "And exactly how do you plan to make use of Elise?" he asked.

"Well, I was thinking, you see, that if she were to come and stay with me, it would be far better, far, far better than Aunt Lavinia—my late husband's sister, you see—Christian Woodville's aunt, who is a dragon of a woman, and she hates dogs, and it would be simply dreadful! But if Elise were living with me, you see, Aunt Lavinia would not come from Bath, and I could make Elise all the crack also, and she could go to Almack's, and meet gentlemen and—we would be quite a comparison, you know, I so fair and Elise so dark, and Brandamore was promised to assist me—"

M. le Comte tried, without much success, to sort out these various statements, but Lady Charlotte, having decided that all was settled in that quarter, rose from her chair, "Anyway, Christian will be there, also, to keep an eye on both of us, and if she is in the least unhappy, she can come back to you! Oh, this is of all things famous, M'sieu Auguste! What fun it will be to present Elise to society! I'll wager you that I shall have her married to—to a duke within a twelve-month!"

"But she will need clothes, and—I am not at all sure that Elise will consent to—that is—her painting!" M. le Comte sputtered.

Lady Charlotte blinked. "Oh, M'sieu! You are a very warm man! Why, all the world knows that you sold Lord Elgin that whatdoyecallit—Rembrandt? Bosk—no, Bosch, for thousands of pounds! Besides, I am as rich as a golden ball now, and if you won't allow your own niece the chance to see a bit of the world—the world to which her birth entitles her—then, I shall, certainly!"

This was too much for the man who prided himself in starting from nothing to provide something for his nephew and niece. Drawing himself up to his full height, he looked down upon the female he had known since she was a schoolgirl. "Charlotte! If Elise wants this—this Almack's, this ton life, and your stepson is agreeable, then she shall not need to beg money from you! Call upon her tomorrow morning and lay the proposition before her, and if she is agreeable, why, she may spend a thousand pounds upon her clothes if she wishes. But I warn you, Elise has no taste for the social life! To paint—that is all she cares about!"

"And Noel," Lady Charlotte added thoughtfully. "You say that you were hoping that Christian would use his influence to procure a post for Noel?"

She had hit upon Comte Auguste's blind spot. "Yes," he sighed.

Lady Charlotte nodded brightly, extending her hand. "So, it is settled then! I am sure that Christian will agree, for he is excessively in aversion to Aunt Lavinia also! So you need only to put a word in Elise's ear, and between the two of us, we shall each have what we need, no?"

"*Oui,*" Comte Auguste sighed again. As he watched the door close behind Lady Charlotte, he wondered again how any female so patently scatterbrained could always manage to have her own way through the medium of logic.

Chuckling to himself, Comte Auguste returned to his study of the landscape miniatures.

The reunion of the Pellerin family that night on Half Moon Street might have been a completely joyous occasion if Noel, already exhausted from the long journey, had not imbibed too much wine with dinner.

All through the meal, he sullenly watched and listened as his sister and his uncle excitedly forecast his future; Christian Woodville, Lord Ramsey, Mr. Pitt—these gentlemen could and would

agree to interview him for a position in the Foreign Office. Of course, at first, it would not be
too much, but he would surely rise on his merits
—and on and on in this vein until the boy could
stand it no longer.

"Will you stop!" he shouted, cutting through
their dialogue, his dark face flushed and sullen.
His fist crashed onto the table. "You speak as
if—as if being a secretary were a noble position
for a man of my birth! Yes! A secretary! That is
what I shall be, no better than a clerk in a count-
inghouse!"

"Noel—" Elise cautioned.

"No! I will not be quiet!" Noel shouted, disre-
garding the stern look which passed across his
uncle's countenance. "I, I am Prince Pierre Guil-
laume Noel Auguste Pellerin! I—I should have
my estates, my chateaus, my rightful place in the
world! That is what you have both been forever
telling me that I was born for, not to be a secretary to some doddering peer!"

"You've had too much wine, Noel—" Comte
Auguste said soothingly.

But Noel merely sank down into his chair, his
dark eyes glittering in the candlelight. "No!" he
repeated. "I will not! I will not, I tell you!
Napoleon is calling us all to come home to
France, to have our lands and our estates returned to us! And you—you two are such fools
that you won't go!"

"Home to a country you barely know! That I

barely know!" Elise said, forcing herself to remain calm. So many times, this same argument. "Noel, you don't remember—you cannot remember what it was like—the streets, red with blood, the screaming, the sound of the heads as they fell from the block to the ground—"

"That's over and done with! Old Robespierre and poor Marat are gone and the emperor has restored order— In France, I should have my rightful place—"

"Kissing the boots of a Corsican upstart!" Auguste exclaimed. *"Mon cher* Noel, you are but a boy. You do not understand—"

"I understand that you would have me sent out like an apprentice, when, in France, I would live like a king! My birthright, uncle! My birthright!"

"Your birthright was destroyed by the follies of your ancestors," Auguste said quietly.

"Here, now! Such talk of treason as I hear in this room!" said a familiar voice from the doorway.

"Emile!" Elise said in a low voice, exchanging a glance with her uncle.

Emile Bertraine strolled into the room. He was tall and thin, with quick, foxlike eyes that betrayed the languidness of his casual manners. He was dressed in evening clothes, which accented the natural pallor of his skin. His glance, amused and somehow greedy, swept across the Pellerin family. Auguste was sagging in his chair, his eyes dark with his concern for Noel, who had risen from his place, his napkin still clutched in his hand. Before him, the spreading wine stain on the white linen tablecloth looked like blood. And lastly, Emile's glance rested upon Elise, and the greed in his eyes deepened.

He bowed in her direction. "Good evening, Elise. I understand that we shall have the pleasure of seeing more of you, now that you will be residing in London. M. le Comte, I bid you good evening. Noel, Noel, *mon copain,* is this any way to speak before your elders? That is precisely the sort of talk that could get you into deep trouble, my friend!"

Noel's shoulders relaxed slightly in his green velvet coat. He looked down at his hand. "I— I'm sorry, uncle," he muttered sullenly. "Sorry, Elise. I—I know that you want to do the best for me, but—"

"There, there," Auguste said soothingly, glad to see that once again Emile Bertraine had exercised his usual salubrious effect upon his young friend. "Come, now, no more talk of Napoleon and France! Emile, will you have a glass of wine with us? Some dinner?"

Emile shook his head as much as his shirt points would allow him to do so. "Ah, no, no. As a matter of fact, I merely dropped by to see if I could take Noel out upon the town! I've already dined, and I'm on my way to Boodle's. Do to give him a taste of the town, I think. But one thing, *mes amis*, if you must argue about Boney, it's best that you do it in French—at least when the servants are within listening distance. Wouldn't do for anyone to think that we were all sympathizers of the Little Corsican, would it?"

Noel's mood suddenly shifted again. "Oh, Boodle's! I should like to go there! They say that the duke of York gambles with golden guineas!"

Emile laughed softly. "And I have managed, from time to time, to gamble some of them away from him. Perhaps I will be lucky tonight! Come, M. le Comte, and give your consent! *Notre petit prince* should acquire a bit of town bronze after all. Do him good after having his head buried in the books for so long!"

Elise and her uncle exchanged a glance.

"Very well, very well," Auguste sighed, "but try to be in by a reasonable hour. Emile, you will see that he's not taken to one of those hells of yours?"

Bertraine laughed, twirling his walking stick in his hand. "Who could be safer to be with than a Captain Sharp?" He laughed. "Come, Noel, take that face off and change your clothes!"

As the lad ran up the stairs to put on suitable raiment for a young gentleman's night on the town, Emile settled himself comfortably into a chair near Elise. "Thank you!" she told him in a low voice. "Noel never seems to listen to Uncle or me as well as he attends to you. You will try to make him understand that it is most important that he pursue a career, will you not?"

Emile shook his head, a lazy smile playing over his features. His eyes surveyed Elise in her plain cambric gown. "If only I could exert some sort of influence over you, *ma petite*," he sighed half-seriously.

Elise laughed and threw back her head. "Oh, you know very well that no one has the least influence over me, Emile! Besides, I know too well your appreciation for lovely females as well as the turn of the ivories!"

Bertraine clucked his tongue, accepting the glass that the *comte* offered him. "Such language! Hardly fit for a princess! Ivories, indeed!"

"And gambling and wenching, I suppose, are suitable occupations for a chevalier!" she retorted with easy camaraderie.

Bertraine shook his head, leaning closer to both the Pellerins. "I slipped across the Channel last week," he said in rapid French, conveying secrecy with a slight gesture of his head toward the footman at the sideboard, "just for a look about, and a visit to a most delectable lady, who, unfortunately, is married to one of Napoleon's aides-de-camp. Met her during the Peace, at the Tuilleries."

"You went to France?" Auguste replied in the same low tone, bending forward. "How does one—?"

Bertraine studied his well-manicured nails. "It ain't hard—Cornwall and Brittany, it's all the same between the free traders, no matter who's in power in London and Paris. Grease the right fist, and you're aboard a fishin' smack! Ain't the best form of travel in the world, but it's good enough for brandy and silks and gentlemen who visit married ladies on the seaside for their health." He grinned suddenly, then allowed his thin face to turn serious again. "What Noel says is very true, you know—Bonaparte's quite anxious to establish his own empire, handing out titles and parcels of countries to those relations of his, and he's asking us to come back to lend himself cachet! Pompous little ass! Promising a restoration of lands and titles if you'll give him allegiance!"

Elise looked at her uncle. His face was dark, and slowly he shook his head from side to side. "No! Never! Not even if that fat fool at Hartwell were to ascend the throne of France would I return. What has happened once may happen again, Emile, and well you know that. England has been good to me. I have prospered here beyond my own expectations. I have made a life for myself and my brother's children. Whatever I would go back for, it would be gone. . . . My friends, my family—they are all dead. France is the past, England is the present. And especially now, with that Corsican upstart, a thousand times worse than poor silly Louis and Antoinette."

Emile shrugged. "There are many in St. George's Fields who think differently, you know. They have not fared so well here as you have, M'sieu Auguste."

"And you?" Elise asked.

"Me? I am a simple soldier of fortune. I can turn my ivories wherever there is a gaming table and a pigeon to be plucked," he replied with a grin. "You know that I care only for chance— and myself."

"Come, Emile, let's be off!" Noel cried, running down the stairs, still adjusting his neck cloth, his cloak thrown over his arm.

Emile rose from the table. "When I go again, I shall see if I can win an Ingres or a David on a turn of the cards for you, my fair Elise!" he promised lightly, his hand resting on hers for one second before he was gone. "Oh, and by the way—you will give my regards to that old dragon of yours, Yvonne? Tell her I kiss her rosy cheeks!" His voice drifted lightly up the hallway.

Auguste leaned back in his chair. From an inner pocket he removed his snuffbox and inhaled a deep pinch. After he had blown his nose and adjusted his waistcoat to make allowances for a fine dinner, he regarded Elise thoughtfully.

How many years has she been wearing that plain old cambric gown? he wondered. And when had she started to place that badge of spin-

sterhood, a cap, upon her curls? It seemed as if
only yesterday she had been a little girl, and
now, she was regarding herself as an old maid.
Perhaps, just perhaps, in his ambitions for Noel,
he had ignored Elise's needs, just a trifle. Of
course, as long as she could dabble with her
paints, she never complained, but still— She was
a fetching enough female, and certainly it would
be a true sin not to place her in the way of mas-
culine company. . . . Look at her, the wine in
his head told him, sitting there daydreaming over
the tablecloth, her mind given over, no doubt, to
grinding pigments or making brushes, when she
should be thinking of clothes and balls and
dances!

As if she had read his thoughts, Elise looked
up and smiled affectionately at her uncle.

He cleared his throat. "Speaking of dragons,
my dear," he began, well aware that Elise could
be led but not driven, "you will never guess who
paid a call upon me today! Lady Charlotte St.
Ives! Of course, she is Mrs. Woodville, now, but
so young and a widow!"

Elise's face brightened. "Oh, yes! I must see
her! I wrote to tell her that I would be living in
London now."

Auguste nodded. "She, er, called upon me to
ask my opinion of your coming to stay with her
for an extended visit. It seems that her stepson
Christian Woodville feels that she needs a chaperone now that she is out of her mourning for

old Mr. Woodville. There are only seven years between them, and he feels that their continued residence in the same household would give rise to unsuitable gossip if she does not have a female companion to lend her company. . . ."

"Aunt Aurelia!" Elise exclaimed. "Of course! Poor Charlotte, she was ever terrified of Miss Woodville! And Mr. Woodville proposes no doubt to import Miss Woodville from Bath unless I am persuaded to come and lend assistance!" She shook her head. "Oh, I had thought my days of taking Charlotte out of the basket were long over!" She laughed, touching her uncle's arm.

He nodded. "There are, of course, certain advantages to staying with Charlotte that you would not have here, you know. You would be able to go about a great deal more and meet people of your own age and go to parties and such like. I daresay it would be far better than keeping house for an old man like me!"

Since Comte Auguste employed a large and skillful staff to attend to his every need, Elise blinked, but bit back her teasing laughter. At first, she was inclined to toss off the proposal with the light remark that no doubt Charlotte would be married again within a twelvemonth, and that her uncle needed her much more, particularly now that Noel would be living with him. Noel. Of course.

"And what does Christian Woodville have to

say about all this? Doubtless he is less than thrilled to have an insignificant creature such as myself in his household! The only time he ever deigned to look at me, he told me that I painted like a man!"

Auguste narrowed his eyes. Although this was said in a cool tone he could detect a trace of very real resentment underlying her tone. "I am certain that he meant it as a compliment, Elise," he hastened to say soothingly. "After all, Woodville is a very influential man, and a very strong critic of the arts! Only think, to live with his collection would be a very good experience for you. . . ."

"So would living in the National Gallery!!" Elise retorted. "Poor, dear Charlotte, to be under the same roof with that man! He must thwart her at every turn, he so serious and she so gay, but no, I do not think so. You know that I would only find myself excessively uncomfortable with Charlotte's fashionable friends, and they with me. . . ." She dipped her finger, in a most unladylike manner, into her wineglass and traced the lip of the crystal with her finger. "And to be in the same house with a man who says that I paint like a man, as if that were a compliment, as if Miss Kauffmann and Mrs. Cosway, Miss Moser and Lady Diana Beauclerk were all— Oh, insufferable! Uncle, now is as good a time as any for you to come and see my new paintings! I think you will find them most interesting!"

The problems of Lady Charlotte and Christian

Woodville were swiftly forgotten as uncle and niece descended into the long gallery of the house. Calling for knife and scissors from a footman, they attacked the muslin wrappings of Elise's canvases. When all ten stood against the wall, Elise hovered over her uncle's shoulder as he studied the series of landscapes. He was forced to admit that she had learned her lessons well and worked hard at her craft. In her brush, she had captured the essence of shadows and light that played across the four seasons of the countryside; her colors were rendered with truth and simple beauty. But even more, she had, it seemed to him, found something else, some deeper expression of time and space in her well-rendered pastoral scenes. He took a deep breath.

"It's no good, then?" Elise asked, unable to bear the silence any longer. "I knew that that cerulean was too blue for those skies—"

Auguste held up his hand, then placed it upon his heart. "Elise, you are a genius," he said simply. "You are a real artist. It can no longer be denied." There were tears of pride in his eyes, and he was forced to blow his nose. "Your talent—that we must have come through what we have come through in order that your gifts be exposed to the world—to lose your parents, to leave *la belle France*, all of it, all of it is worth it, if only for these canvases!"

Elise clapped her hands together. "Then you will give me a show, Uncle?"

"I will give you the main salon of my gallery!" he promised. "If only—if only you were a man, Elise, what genius I could seize upon for you, what successes you could have!"

"Oh, Uncle!" she replied, taking his hand in hers. "I have even resolved that prejudice! If you will notice, each canvas is signed only E. M. d'Angelle! M. d'Angelle, you see, is a very reclusive artist, and he abhors public gatherings, and he is as eccentric as—as, oh, Woodville himself, and never sees anyone! Oh, Uncle, do you understand? Paintings by Miss Pellerin are very pretty, but they will never never be accepted in the same way that paintings by a M. d'Angelle will be received!"

The comte was forced to agree with the truth of this statement, if not with the actual honesty of its practice. "How will you feel, Elise, when this mythical d'Angelle receives the accolades which rightfully belong to you?" he demanded sternly.

Elise's lips turned upward slightly. "As if I have pulled off a great coup, Uncle! Imagine how much of a fool such noble critics and Mr. Woodville will feel when I declare myself as a woman! Uncle, do not tell me it is not fair, for it will be honest, in time, I assure you! I only wish to prove my point that a woman can paint as well as any man!"

"But Woodville can do so much for your brother!"

"But he is not the only one," Elise countered. "Uncle, please, do this one thing for me, and I shall never ask for anything else! I shall even go to visit with Charlotte for a space and be very nice to Mr. Woodville, if only you will agree!"

Reluctantly, because he felt a certain sense of guilt about his treatment of Elise, prompted in the main by Lady Charlotte's remarks, Auguste gave in. "Oh, very well," he agreed, throwing up his hands. "But I warn you, Elise, this idea is folly!"

"Oh, Uncle, you are the positively best uncle in the world!" Elise exclaimed.

Chapter Four

At that very same time, Lady Charlotte happened to encounter her stepson on the stairs as both were bound out the door.

Mr. Woodville, wearing his evening clothes and his diplomatic sash, appraised Charlotte with critical eye. "You ain't going out in that, are you, Charlotte?" he asked her, his tone of disapproval slightly mellowed by a faint glint of amusement in his eye.

Lady Charlotte's haughty dresser, Elder, trailing behind her mistress with cloak and gloves, gave a disapproving sniff, since it had taken her nearly two hours to arrange milady's toilette into the currently fashionable rage for disarray.

Lady Charlotte cast a look down at her thin, muslin ball-gown, a devastatingly simple confection of clinging white relieved by gold bands of embroidered Greek keys at hem and sleeve. About the high waist, Elder had tied a golden cord, and the catch train Lady Charlotte had slung carelessly over one gloved arm was also of golden braid. In her fair curls, dressed in the style designated at the Athena, several tall white ostrich plumes fluttered high above her head. The slimmest gold sandals and an ivory fan depicting scenes from the *Judgment of Paris* completed her ensemble.

She allowed her lashes to flutter. "You don't like it, Christian?"

"Complete, I am sure, to a shade!" he responded dryly. "But I am certain that you will freeze to death before you arrive at your destination!"

"Oh, no, we are only to Lady Sefton's, and George always keeps an excessively warm lap-robe in his carriage. He is very scrupulous about his comfort, you know," she added complacently. "And you?"

"Quite a very much duller affair, I imagine! Melbourne's party for the Swedish consul! I daresay it will be politics all evening, but I'd rather there than one of Sefton's crushes!"

Lady Charlotte rapped his shoulder with her fan playfully. "You are the most odious beast in nature, Christian!" she said without rancor. "Oh, and by the way, I have found a suitable duenna, so there is really no need to write to Aunt Aurelia! My old school friend Elise Pellerin will be coming to stay with me for a while—Miss Copplestone's School, you know! She is quite respectable, and two whole years older than I!"

"What! Comte Pellerin's daughter?" Christian responded. "The little drab who paints?"

"Niece, you goose, niece. Do be an angel and be kind to her. Brandamore and I intend to bring her into the way of society. Imagine, the poor thing has been buried in Oxford all these years, bearing her brother company while he was at university! *Very* dull! It is my intention to put her in the way of a little enjoyment, so it shall all work out in a perfectly admirable manner, do you not think?"

Mr. Woodville shrugged indifferently. "No doubt. You must do as you please! I am sure that she will be far better company than Aunt Aurelia!"

Declining with rather more firmness than the occasion commanded Lady Charlotte's invitation to take him up to Grosvenor Square in Brandamore's carriage, Woodville graciously bid Lady Charlotte a good evening, grunted in barely concealed contempt at Brandamore's black silk waistcoat with diamond buttons and strolled out into the cool evening air.

It was several minutes before he was able to bring Miss Pellerin's person into focus in his mind, and the image he retained of her during one brief meeting in her uncle's house. It seemed to him that she had been a rather tall creature of no particular originality. Indeed, the word *drab* was a suitable appellation, for she had been wearing a colorless gown, and her hair had been done into two simple bands. She had been working on a small gouache cartoon, as he recalled, that betrayed some talent rather above the norm for female dilettantism. Beyond a feeling that she was rather serious and possessed little conversation outside the sphere of art, he really could not recall any distinguishing feature. He inhaled deeply of the cold night air. In short, he thought, she would make an admirably repressive companion for Charlotte's too-high spirits. Although, he thought, what Lord Brandamore would make of her was beyond his guess. Having satisfied himself upon the score of his very young stepmother's propriety, he immediately cast all thoughts of Miss Pellerin out of his mind and proceeded on his way.

Lord Brandamore had been awakened from a profound repose at what he uncivilly informed his valet was a most unnatural hour of ten in the morning. The dire emergency which had prompted this most professional gentleman's gentleman to violate his employer's inviolate rule about being disturbed before noon was a communication which Coe, the bearer, had assured him came from the pen of Lady Woodville and was most urgent indeed.

Therefore, the mood in which he presented himself at Number 16 was not of the best. Although he deemed that the situation must indeed be one of life and death for his cousin to thus preemptively demand his presence, he had been annoyed to find that his concentration had been so disturbed as to make the arrangement of his neck cloth a fraction short of its usual perfection, and these two irritating problems were on his mind when Basile ushered him into the morning room.

At first, his impulse was to release a blistering tirade upon the head of his hapless and inconsiderate cousin, for the scene which presented itself to his eye did not, at first glance, seen to be in any way disastrous: Two females who have not seen one another for several years, seated upon a sofa, chattering animatedly about persons and places totally alien to him, punctuated by peals of laughter and affectionate embraces, after all, is hardly cause for alarm. It was only when Lady Charlotte jumped up in a rustle of eggshell lace morning dress and he was fully able to perceive that the other lady must be none other than Miss Pellerin that he decided to forgive Charlotte, for this, indeed, was a situation in which only his fine hand would be called upon to allay the danger.

He barely heard his cousin making the necessary introductions, so overcome were his sensibilities by the sight of an olive-complected female wearing a linsey gown of a particularly unflattering shade of tan; but, as if he stood outside of his own impeccable person, he heard himself making the proper responses, all the while sizing up the possibilities; for it was one of Lord Brandamore's indefatigable rules that any female could be dressed to advantage, given taste, fashion and, of course, a great deal of the blunt. Miss Pellerin was tall—this was a point in her favor; she was dark—a point against her, but of no consequence, for he believed that he could contrive to stem the current rage for Dresden blondes; she carried herself well—a point for her; her nails were neat, but badly groomed—a point against; her figure was good—a point for her; her nose was far too long to be considered classical—a point against. . . . Tears almost rose in his eyes, and his heart soared, for before him lay his greatest challenge. Could he, would he, rise to it? For a moment, he doubted even his own powers, but a certain pleading look of complete faith lay in his cousin's eyes, and one simple word formed upon his lips.

"Madame Celeste's."

Miss Pellerin regarded him as if he were mad, but Lady Charlotte clapped her hands together in relieved delight.

As if in a dream, Elise's vague protests were ignored as Lady Charlotte arranged her plain pelisse about her shoulders and she was borne away by her two companions to an elegant establishment on Milson Street where a sharp-faced female of almost awesome haughtiness took one look at her and immediately entered into deep conference with Lady Charlotte and Lord Brandamore, during which such mysterious utterings as "blond lace", "Venus points," "India crêpe," and "celestial blue" drifted to her ears, while an openly curious assistant took her measure.

Madame Celeste murmured in French, Lord Brandamore mopped his brow, Lady Charlotte fingered delicate fabrics with the practiced skill of a mercer, and Elise sat, almost completely entranced, as gown after beautiful gown was brought out of the mysterious workrooms of Madame Celeste's *atelier* for her inspection. Or, rather the inspection of Lord Brandamore and Lady Charlotte, since no one seemed concerned with her opinons on all of this.

When Elise ventured a faint protest, Lady Charlotte merely kissed her forehead and assured her that now that she was in London, where things were done quite differently, it would be most necessary for her to be properly attired. So overwhelming were the events of that morning, Elise allowed herself to be led into a dressing room where she was outfitted, like a doll, with more than twenty dresses, then brought forth for the critical inspection of Brandamore and Lady Charlotte.

It was well into the afternoon when the trio left the modiste's shop, burdened down beneath the weight of several bandboxes. Their next stop was the millinery shop of the very tonnish Mrs. Fletcher, where caps, bonnets and hats of every description were fitted upon Miss Pellerin's head. She revived from her shock of the morning so far as to plead for a particularly unusual cottage hat of chipstraw, ornamented with pink rosettes and ribands. This notion was firmly removed from her head by Lord Brandamore, who informed her that with her dark complexion pink was absolute disaster, and Lady Charlotte, who perceived that she would look a quiz; however, since the same hat looked quite admirable upon her fair curls, while a bronze toque of silk and brocade trimmed with two very dashing ostrich feathers of pomona green for which Lady Charlotte had developed a tendre was pronounced by Lord Brandamore to be all the thing upon Miss Pellerin's dark locks, a trade was made, and both ladies were satisfied.

After that, there was a visit to Mr. Clarke, The Prince's Own Shoemaker, for slippers, jean half-boots for walking, leather boots for riding in the park, sandals with soles as thin as rice paper for dancing, and a pair of mules to be worn in the boudoir; a stop at Jetson's, the mantua maker on Oxford Street, produced several pairs of gloves, a set of ostrich plumes in every shade of the rainbow, some lace mitts and two morning caps, not to mention camisoles, corselets and silk stockings.

It was well past teatime when Lord Brandamore pronounced himself satisfied that every outer accouterment of a fashionable lady had been obtained.

Surveying Miss Pellerin up and down, he nodded with complete self-satisfaction. "Said I couldn't do it! By God, if I could turn that Rampling cit into a countess, there's no limit to what I can do with Miss Pellerin! Except, my dear, never wear pink in any shade, if you wish to be complete!" He nodded brightly at Elise, who was forced, not for the first time, to suppress a gurgle of laughter. She found it extremely hard to believe Lord Brandamore was leading the beau of the ton, but then again, she had not as yet been exposed to that particular face of society. "Charl', you set Elder at her hair tonight. Can't venture out to the opera lookin' like that. I'll set Sally Jersey upon the Almack's vouchers, if you please. Remember, Miss Pellerin, no pink! Charl', set me down at Albemarle Street. I simply must have an hour's lay-down upon my bed or I shall look a fright tonight!" With those words, he closed his eyes, crossed his arms across his waistcoat and went into a reverie so profound that it took the point of Lady Charlotte's parasol to prod him back into life at his destination.

"If I may say so," Elise confided to her friend when Lord Brandamore had taken himself off, "your cousin is a trifle eccentric, is he not?"

Lady Charlotte, who had never considered this before, blinked her eyes and nibbled thoughtfully at the tip of her white kid glove for a second. "Why, I do suppose he is, Elise," she responded at last. "But you must know that he has devoted his life to taste, at the sacrifice of everything else. His mother, you see, was known to faint while she was carrying him at the sight of his father in a cherry-red brocade waistcoat; so perhaps that *may* explain it. . . ." She brightened, patting her friend's hand. "Whatever, he likes you, and he often does not like anyone! And George is very fashionable, you know; so that must signify!"

Miss Pellerin, not yet completely understanding the schemes which had been laid for her future by her well-wishers, merely smiled encouragingly at her scatterbrained friend.

But when the various bandboxes and packages were piled into her room by the footmen, she began to understand the dire consequences of her day's expedition. "Dear Lord, Charlotte," she exclaimed, wringing her hands, "I must take these back—at least some of them."

"But why?" asked Lady Charlotte, unwrapping an exquisite evening dress of ivory peau-de-soir with a half-skirt of banded bronze sarcenet for the critical inspection of Elder. Both mistress and maid, unaccustomed to measures of frugality, stared at Miss Pellerin uncomprehend-ingly as she cast herself upon the boudoir chair in the throes of anguish.

"I have overextended my uncle's credit, I am certain! He said that I was to buy a few things to make myself presentable, but this" —her hand swept over the alps of dresses, shoes, hats and accessories— "this is far too much!"

While Lady Charlotte remonstrated with her friend by pointing out that each garment was far too precious to be parted with, Miss Elder pro-vided a subtle distraction by arranging Miss Pel-lerin's dark locks in the style known as the Athene.

With Lady Charlotte and Elder both working in attendance, Miss Pellerin's new toilette was soon arranged, and she was brought to view her-self in Lady Charlotte's pier glass.

Miss Pellerin's reactions were so spontane-ously heartrending that even the cool Miss Elder was forced to smile.

Elise's hand reached out to touch the glass as if she could not quite believe that it reflected her own image. The female she beheld certainly had her features and figure, but where in this ele-gant young female was the mouselike creature she had so recently been? With the skillful aid of

Elder's curling iron, her bands of dark hair had been transformed into a riot of glossy curls which framed her heart-shaped face (her natural color heightened ever so subtly by a judicious application of rouge); her shoulders and bosom were shown to advantage by the rather dashing cut of an evening dress of hussar beige banded round waist and hem with delicate ruching of blond lace and highlighted by the newly fashionable bishop sleeves, slashed back to reveal the same froth of blond lace, and banded with cords of bronze silk. Into her hair, Elder had braided a length of this same bronze cord, ornamented with one small rosette. A pair of flat ivory slippers striped with pomona green, and a small silk fan completed this toilette.

Lady Charlotte clapped her hands. "Perfect!" she exclaimed. "Nothing could be better, if you were to wear my beaver opera-cloak, Lord, Elise, I should hardly believe it was you!"

"Nor I," Elise murmured, turning this way and that to watch the silk shimmer beneath the light. She smiled, and the ravishing creature in the mirror smiled back. Miss Pellerin, for the first time in her life, began to understand the possibilities of her own beauty.

"Now, my love, do you go on downstairs while Elder finishes dressing me," Lady Charlotte commanded her friend, giving her an airy kiss upon her cheek. "I daresay George will be along directly, and I daresay he will want to see his creation immediately."

Feeling rather as if she had stepped into a dream from which she did not wish to awaken, Miss Pellerin descended the steps to the green salon. Coe, at his place in the hallway, quite forgot himself as far as to stare openmouthed at the vision which made its way across his line and into the chamber. It was quite some seconds before he was able to divine that this beauty was the French person my lady had taken under her wing, so great was her transformation. Or at least that was the story with which he regaled Basile when the butler brought up Mr. Woodville's sherry.

Mr. Woodville's chambers were in the wing opposite Lady Charlotte's, an arrangement which suited them both. He spent the afternoon writing various dispatches, totally oblivious to the miracle being wrought beneath his own roof. When Greenough, his valet, informed him that it was time to change for his engagement at White's, he was still absorbed in Foreign Office business, and went so far as to carry his document case into the green salon to pursue matters further while he awaited his dinner.

Lady Charlotte was not known for the brevity of making her toilette, and Miss Pellerin soon found herself bored with such literature as the *Lady's Magazine* to be found in the room. There was a desk in the corner, armed with paper and ink, and it was not long before her fingers sought entertainment in making a sketch of the Fragonard which hung above the desk.

So absorbed was she in this occupation that she did not hear Mr. Woodville make his entrance, nor see his brows rise slightly at the sight of a strange female, very elegantly attired, studiously given over to the study of what he considered to be one of the lesser works of his collection. Nonetheless, he was intrigued enough to steal quietly up behind this lady and observe her work.

What he saw was so far beyond the normal run of female dabbling, so skillful and pointed a study of the oil, that he was surprised into a closer examination, and his sleek head was almost upon Miss Pellerin's shoulder before she sensed his presence. "Oh!" she exclaimed, turning to the sight of Mr. Woodville's handsome features so very close to her own. The pen rolled out of her surprised hand and might have irrevocably stained her dress had not his hand swiftly captured the writing instrument as it trailed across the blotter. Since she had the same idea, his hand captured her own for a few brief seconds over the quill.

"Allow me," he said smoothly, extricating the instrument from her grasp without staining her fingers. "I did not mean to startle you, ma'am, but your drawing was quite above the ordinary, and art is one of what my stepmother calls my ruling passions, Miss, er—"

Elise, driving down with a great deal of effort the rosy flush that suffused her cheeks, finished his sentence flatly, rising from the chair. "—Pellerin, sir. I believe we have already met."

"Miss Pellerin?" Mr. Woodville said in tones so patently unbelieving that the flush rose again to her cheeks. "I—that is—surely you cannot be the Miss Pellerin who is the niece of Comte Auguste Pellerin?"

"I have the honor to be that person, Mr. Woodville," Elise replied, barely able to suppress a smile at his unbelieving expression. "Surely you must recall our meeting a few years ago at my uncle's home?" she added mischievously.

Mr. Woodville recollected himself with admirable swiftness. "Of course, Miss Pellerin. How very silly of me not to recall you."

"I have changed a great deal," Elise suggested, her eyes twinkling. She was beginning to find that she liked her new self very much.

"Indeed, Miss Pellerin," Mr. Woodville agreed, with a long look that took in everything between the russet curls surrounding her piquant face to the tiny brown and green slippers on her feet. It was almost impossible for him to believe that this was the same Miss Pellerin he had shrugged off so lightly that previous evening as a female of no consequence. "I am given to understand that you will be visiting with Charlotte for a space. She had given me to understand that you would be chaperoning her—but now I think that I must provide a chaperone for both of you."

This was said in such good humor that Elise was forced to accept the compliment with a blushing denial. "Indeed, sir," she told his top button from beneath lowered eyelashes, "I am far beyond the age of needing a duenna. You must rest assured that I will lend Charlotte company. Indeed, it is a pleasure to be installed in a house with such a renowned collection."

Mr. Woodville's eyes gleamed appreciatively at the mention of his ruling passion. "And do you still paint, Miss Pellerin? I seem to recall some talents of yours in that direction."

Although nothing Mr. Woodville could utter was more calculated to set Miss Pellerin's hackles up, she hastily recalled that if she desired Mr. Woodville's favor in setting Noel up with the Foreign Office, it would be wise for her to suppress her own feelings. And there was also the matter of the mythical E. M. d'Angelle to be considered; upon that point would she have her revenge on this smiling peer, she thought and made herself shrug one elegant shoulder. "Oh, I do a bit of dabbling, as you can see by this sketch, but lately I have been studying with M. d'Angelle."

"D'Angelle?" Mr. Woodville asked cautiously.

"I am not familiar with the name. Is he with the Royal Academy?"

Elise shook her head. "Oh no, M. d'Angelle is rather reclusive. In fact," she added, warming to the theme, "my uncle feels very lucky to have ten of his canvases to exhibit, for you must know that he burns everything that does not exactly please him—and nothing pleases him."

Mr. Woodville looked intrigued. "Since you know that I am by way of being a collector, you must know that I pride myself on being cognizant of all the modern artists. And yet this d'Angelle is someone I have never heard of."

"Oh," said Elise airily, "I believe both Egremont and Beckford have examples of his work, but he is not quite to everyone's taste. Landscapes and natural realism, you know. He is a great believer in Rousseau."

Since Lord Egremont and Sir William Beckford were amongst the premiere patrons and collectors, Mr. Woodville felt a slight sting of jealousy that they had acquired paintings by this artist of whom he had never heard mention. He shook his head, clearly puzzled that this light of the art world had escaped his attention.

"Oh, of course you would not just hear of him, you know. He is not RA, in fact his work is quite radical, I believe—even Billy Turner says so," Elise continued blithely, enjoying her little revenge on the man who had remarked that *she painted like a man*. "In fact, my uncle considered

himself quite lucky when M. d'Angelle consented
to allow him to show his work at the gallery.
Uncle believes that he will be quite the next
thing. Of course, M. d'Angelle is very shy and
odiously eccentric and refuses to meet any of his
admirers, and I feel quite fortunate to study with
him—when he decides that he wishes to have a
pupil, of course." Feeling that she had taken this
theme quite far enough, she swept a hand about
the salon. "But you must tell me about your collection, sir. It is considered, my uncle says, one
of the best in England, and he said I must in particular pay attention to your fine Italian masters."

Woodville would much have preferred to pursue the mysterious M. d'Angelle, for his pride
was severely tried that a man who prided himself
upon his collection of contemporary artists
would be so behind-hand in the latest sensation;
but he was definitely not adverse to showing an
attractive female through the long gallery, and
with a sweep of his hand, he bowed her toward
the door.

Miss Pellerin, however, was not the usual female tourist to coo in rapture over chubby-faced
madonnas and sinister merchant princes of
the Renaissance. Her *cicerone,* conducting her
through the various chambers which housed his
works, found her appreciation to be shrewdly
knowledgeable, and her questions and observa-
tions to be those of a trained and educated artist.
For her, there was nothing of the dilettante soci-

ety deb's fashionable viewing; in their tour, it was clear to Mr. Woodville that here was a female who could appreciate and converse upon a topic dear to his own heart.

The consequence of this was that by the time they had wended their way back to the green salon, Woodville and Miss Pellerin found themselves upon charity with one another in the matter of painting. When Lady Charlotte, released from Elder's ministrations, came tripping down the steps, a vision of blond beauty in a peach jaconet evening dress with a silver lamé overslip and a banding of silver lace down the front and hem, her small sleeves bounding up her round arms with the same fabric, and a wreath of myrtle holding her fair tresses in the style of Artemis, her famous diamond and pearl collar set about her exquisite neck, and silver sandals upon her feet, a silver shawl negligently draped about her arms, she paused thoughtfully at the sight of the two dark heads so close together, examining the brushstrokes of an *atelier Leonardo*.

A smile played about her lips for a second before she rustled across the room toward them. "There you both are! Woodville, do you make yourself known to Miss Pellerin? Very good, you are acquainted, of course," she said in her breathy little voice, surveying Elise critically. "My dear, I have decided that you must have this shawl of mine—Brandamore says that it will not do for me at all." She proffered a cashmere wrap of lightest ecru, overriding Elise's protestations as she draped it about her friend's shoulders to complete her toilette.

"Well, Christian," Lady Charlotte exclaimed, taking Elise's arm and smiling at her stepson, "Do you approve of my companion? Is not Miss Pellerin by far more preferable than Aunt Lavinia?"

Woodville's blue eyes met Miss Pellerin's darker ones with a secret smile of perfect understanding. "Far better than Lavinia! I only hope we may contrive to entertain her without boring her senseless, as I have been doing for the past half hour."

"Oh, nothing could be more interesting to me than painting," Miss Pellerin replied, but Lady Charlotte squeezed her hand firmly.

"Indeed," she said in her breathless voice, "I thought tonight to take her to the opera—Handel or Mozart or someone, you know, it don't matter, as long as I may contrive to give London a glimpse of Miss Pellerin."

"Rather give Miss Pellerin a glimpse of London," Elise laughed ruefully. "I fear I have never attended an opera at Covent Garden before."

"Really?" Mr. Woodville replied. "I—er, find myself with an engagement to meet Philip Bridges suddenly canceled tonight. So, perhaps, if you do not mind, I will accompany you there?"

Since Woodville was not known for any great

love of this particular form of entertainment, Lady Charlotte merely smiled and answered that he was indeed welcome, if he did not mind an evening in Lord Brandamore's company. With an admirable forbearance he had not previously displayed toward this individual, Woodville replied that it mattered not a whit, and upon this note, they went into dinner.

If Miss Pellerin had expected that the ton would attend a performance of the great Naldi solely to hear the music and see the performance of this mezzo-soprano who had taken the Continent by storn, she was sadly disappointed. In this maiden voyage into the treacherous waters of polite society, she found that one attended the opera for the premier purpose of seeing who else was in attendance, and making certain that one was seen in return. This fact was borne upon her by Lord Brandamore, who raised his quizzing glass as she entered the box in company with the Woodvilles, and pronounced, after a critical survey, that she was something more like, now, and complete to a shade. Lady Charlotte, taking this remark upon herself as a compliment to her own taste, thanked her cousin very much. Anxious lest he should pull the struts away from her budding plans, she immediately recognized Lady Sefton entering her box across the way and insisted that she and Brandamore pay a call upon her friend before the curtain rose, leaving Woodville in charge of Miss Pellerin.

When the cousins had quit the box and were traversing the gallery, Lady Charlotte pulled her cousin aside, drawing his fair head to her own.

"George, what should you think if Miss Pellerin and Christian were to make a match of it?" she demanded breathlessly.

Lord Brandamore, smoothing out the sleeve of his bath suiting coat where Lady Charlotte had grasped his arm, at first made no reply but to call her a silly widgeon to rumple a man's coat. But upon being applied to once again for an opinion, and having all the similarities of interest and taste pointed out to him, he frowned slightly. "I daresay if it could be contrived, it would be an excellent thing. But, damme, Charl', you know as well as I how many females have set their caps upon Christian anytime these past years, and not once has he come up to scratch! Daresay that Miss Pellerin is an agreeable sort of female, if too serious, which I for one must always deplore in women. But, damme, Charl', to be thinkin' of settin' Miss Pellerin up with him— why, both the Gurney chit and that whatyamay-caller Miss Baldistone both tried. What makes you think that Miss Pellerin would succeed where they failed?"

Since the Misses Gurney and Baldistone had both been considered Diamonds of the First Water, Lady Charlotte did pause for a second. But she continued, her spirits in no way diminished, "Well, we shall contrive, I daresay, to make Miss Pellerin, if not precisely a Diamond, at least an Original. It is true that she does not have Miss Gurney's *liveliness,* nor Miss Baldistone's classical beauty, but she does possess a great deal of presence, and she is very pretty!"

"Lacks address," Brandamore said dully. "Come, tuck your arm into mine and let us stroll on, for I see Petersham bearing down upon us, and ten to one he'll want to know where I procured my waistcoat— That is precisely it! The chit lacks address! Doesn't have all the airs and graces! Well, we shall have to put that to rights! Can't go into Almack's with a Friday face, after all, prosin' on about Billy Turner and Miss Kauffmann! Ain't done. She has no small talk! Hmmm . . ."

"I knew you would see it my way," Lady Charlotte smiled up at him sunnily.

"Don't promise miracles, but I suppose we can turn her into something," Brandamore announced gloomily.

Having spent a great deal of time eluding predatory females of just such art and address, Woodville was renewing his acquaintance with Miss Pellerin in a most refreshing fashion. The very lack of artificiality which Brandamore so deplored was found by Woodville to be a definite source of pleasure.

After he had pointed out the various notables filing into their boxes, and given Miss Pellerin a thumbnail biography of each person she might reasonably be expected to encounter on her journeys through the world of ton, they started to cast about the vast hall for unknown faces, inventing histories to fit each party, quite unaware of the attention the lady with Mr. Woodville was causing all about them.

"D'you see that red-faced gentleman, there, with the Lady with the green feathers in her hair?" Mr. Woodville asked his companion, keeping his countenance admirably free of amusement.

Miss Pellerin nodded. "He, of course, is not married to her. In fact, he is her old beau, recently returned from the Indies with a vast fortune in spices, and he is hoping that she will flee with him from her dull and respectable husband."

"Of course, he does not know that she, in turn, is scheming to gain his confidence, before turning him over to the magistrates on charges of free trading—"

"But he will triumph, for in his heart, she is still the sylph of his dreams, rather than the buxom matron we still see, and love will conquer all!"

This portrait so amused both of them that they fell into the giggles together, and were only restrained from further outbursts of humor by an awareness of the presence of others.

Miss Pellerin, who had not been hithertofore aware of the appreciation of the absurd which characterized Woodville's mood, was pleasantly surprised to find herself in complete humor with him.

"I say, Miss Pellerin, there seems to be an acquaintance of yours in the stalls trying to catch your attention," Woodville interrupted their dialogue to point out to his companion.

Elise peered into the sea of faces below, puzzled. When she caught sight of Mr. Noel Pellerin, in evening dress, signaling to her with his program, she turned to Woodville.

"It is my brother, Noel," she said hesitantly, afraid that he might think she was being presumptuous. "Would it be all right if I were to bid him to come to our box?"

"By all means," Woodville agreed expansively. "If I am to be surrounded by Pellerins, it might as well be this evening." He turned Miss Pellerin's program over in his hands, studying her face. "Your uncle mentioned that he hoped I would use my influence to secure your brother some position in the FO. I suppose now is as good a time as any to have a look at the lad."

Elise's face lit up, and the tips of her fingers brushed his arm. "Oh, would you, sir? That is, it would mean so much to my uncle and me. Noel is just down from Oxford, you know, and in addition to speaking three languages fluently, he is also well read in military tactics, international law, history and—"

Woodville held up a hand. "Enough, I beg of

you, Miss Pellerin! We must let even a paragon speak for himself, no matter how fond his sister—"

Noel burst into the box, holding an orange in his hand. In his dark evening clothes, he looked even more handsome, and Woodville was swift to note the resemblance between his companion and her younger sibling, nor was he blind to the swift, protective look which passed over her face as she took in her brother's appearance. If, just for a second, some part of himself wished that she would look at him in that fashion, he swiftly suppressed the thought as being entirely too romantic.

"I say, Elise, I wasn't sure it was really you," Noel burst out at once, without waiting for her to speak. "But don't you look all the crack! The whole place is buzzing with the identity of the Dark Incognita—"

"Noel," Elise stammered, blushing furiously, "please allow me to present you to Mr. Woodville. Mr. Woodville, my brother, Noel Pellerin."

Woodville grasped the youth's hand within his own, his eyes shrewdly taking the young man's measure. "New upon the town?" he drawled with a slight smile.

Noel, recalled to himself, tugged self-consciously at his pearl gray waistcoat and grinned ruefully. "Does it show so much then? I must still look like Johnny Raw!"

Woodville shook his head. "No, your sister has

been priming me. Have you been to see all the sights yet?"

Noel's face lit up. "Have I, then? M'friend Bertraine's been my *cicerone* about the village, sir! I've been to the Daffy Club, and White's, and the Great-Go, The Peerless Pool—in fact, we've just had the most famous sport backstage, Fop's Alley—" His eyes were glittering, and his cheeks were flushed as he recounted his adventures in the tiring room of the opera house.

Woodville, seeing that Miss Pellerin's blush was about to match her sibling's, very kindly reminded Mr. Pellerin that there was a lady present who might object to such talk of opera dancers, nuns and abbesses.

Noel shrugged. "Oh, Elise don't mind that sort of thing, she's m'sister, after all. I say, sir, you're considered a prime whip. Where would a man be going to find himself a bang-up piece of bone and blood to ride in the park?"

"Tattersall's," Mr. Woodville replied without hesitation. "I tell you what, Mr. Pellerin. The curtain's about to go up. I understand that you might be looking for a post in the FO. Why don't you drop around to my offices about eleven tomorrow, and we'll have a talk; then I shall send my own man around to Tat's with you?"

"Oh, that would be famous above all things!" Noel gasped, his newly acquired world-wise manner dropping away from his shoulders. "To go to Tattersall's, I mean."

"And the position, Noel," Elise urged her brother in an undertone.

"What? Oh, yes! Well, that also, of course, Mr. Woodville," he added with less enthusiasm. "I see Bertraine's waving at me. You will excuse me, won't you? Elise, be a good girl now and mind your manners. Don't tease Lady Charlotte," he called, making his bow to Mr. Woodville and disappearing.

"He is very young," she apologized to Mr. Woodville. "I hope you will forgive him his high spirits. I fear he has spent a great deal too much time with his books these past three semesters down."

"Not at all," Woodville said smoothly. "He seems like a fine young man. Perhaps he can be of some use to us. Of course the final decision rests with Pitt, but I can put my word in, you know."

His reward was a grateful smile. Again, the very rational Mr. Woodville found himself thinking that he might have done anything for that elusive expression upon this lady's face, and again, he dismissed the idea as an entirely whimsical aberration.

At that precise moment, Lady Charlotte and Lord Brandamore returned to the box, my lady remarking that she had passed Mr. Pellerin in the gallery, and Lord Brandamore commenting with a great deal of complacency that Lady Sefton had requested Miss Pellerin to visit her box between the acts, a sure sign, if he was not mistaken in Maria, that she would procure the much-desired voucher to Almack's.

At that point, the new gaslights in the pit dimmed and the orchestra stirred the theme. Just before the houselights faded completely away, Elise, watching Noel making his way back to his seat below, caught faint sight of Emile Bertraine's upturned face smiling at her in a most peculiar way. She was about to raise her own hand in salutation when Noel overtook his friend and said something into his ear. Emile, seeming to forget Elise, nodded quite seriously, and the two of them left the theater just as the curtain began to rise.

For the next hour, Elise sat entranced, watching the performance, all thoughts of Emile or indeed anyone else driven from her mind by the costumes and pageantry of Naldi's farewell performance. As the curtain closed over the act, she sighed, and twice had to be recalled by Lady Charlotte to remind her that Lady Sefton awaited her presence in her box.

If Mr. Woodville was expecting to be forced to endure the unrelieved company of Brandamore for the space of the intermission, he was alleviated almost instantly of that belief. One after the other, no less than five bucks of the ton happened to drop by to have a word with one or the other of the two gentleman, seeking to find the true identity of the Dark Incognita upon whom, even at that moment, Lady Sefton was bestowing one of her rare, frosty smiles.

"No use, my boys," Brandamore told them, barely concealing a yawn behind his hand, "she's a friend of Lady Charlotte's, a Miss Pellerin, lately come down from Oxford," was all he would tell Lt. Younger-parrot, Mr. Stanley, or Col. Lord Francis Wolsey.

Christian Woodville, watching these gentlemen with concealed amusement, found himself so completely in accord with Brandamore's reticence that he managed to conduct an almost civil conversation with the famous beau for the full space of five minutes.

After the briefest of conversations with these two gentlemen, each of the bucks suddenly discovered some pressing reason why he must immediately speak to Lady Sefton, and left the box for hers. Unfortunately, by the time they had traversed the theater gallery, Lady Sefton had concluded her interview with Lady Charlotte and Miss Pellerin and the second act was beginning, and those two ladies were wending their way back to their own box again.

"Success!" Lady Charlotte sighed, settling her skirts and shawl into the chair beside Brandamore. "The vouchers come tomorrow!"

"And so, I fear," drawled Brandamore lazily, "a whole host of morning callers. We shall reserve the afternoon, however, for Miss Pellerin's lessons."

Lady Charlotte nodded and settled back into her chair to spend the second act searching the other boxes for signs of her friends and the very latest fashions. Upon chancing to espy either or both of these views in common, she would whisper to Brandamore behind her program in such a way that made Elise, sitting beside her, draw rather more close to Woodville in order to hear the opera.

Mr. Woodville, already bored by the events transpiring upon the stage, and finding the events in the boxes of absolutely no interest whatsoever to himself, took the opportunity to study Miss Pellerin's fine-boned profile and admire her jasmin-based scent.

Quite a fetching little thing, Comte Pellerin's niece, he thought to himself.

Watching her dance at Almack's, perhaps even going so far as to stand up with her once or twice himself, might make an evening at that most inspired gathering quite worth being served only orangeat or champagne punch!

Miss Pellerin, suddenly aware that she was being studied, turned her face toward his.

Slowly, he smiled, and to his great delight, she returned his smile with one of her own.

"Thank you so much for agreeing to have an interview with Noel," she whispered.

"What?" Mr. Woodville, whose thoughts had been in quite another direction, recalled himself instantly. "Oh, yes, of course. Nothing to it," he returned, and focused his attention upon the great mezzo-soprano's aria with rather more devotion than he was feeling.

Chapter Five

"Here's a thing!" Lady Charlotte said from the depths of her pink and white swan bed, shifting the Limoges chocolate pot a little further to the left of her bed tray so that she could fold back the page of that morning's society journal. She closed the lacy ruffles of a peach taffeta bed jacket a little closer over her silken nightdress and glanced at Elise, seated in a very fetching sky blue dressing down at the foot of the bed, reading the *Times*.

Miss Pellerin looked up at her friend from Mr. Hazlitt's rather caustic comments upon the annual exhibition at Somerset House. "I thought you never read anything but the court circular," she said teasingly, helping herself to another cup of chocolate.

Lady Charlotte held the paper quite close to her eyes. "The Incomparable has been joined by a Friend, as might have been seen last night at the opera. Already this *chiaroscuro* Beauty has attracted to herself the appellation, the Dark Incognita, and together, the one Lady so much the perfection of alabaster, the other, so much the apotheosis of ebony, have been declared to be the Contrasts. It is hoped that Society will continue to be adorned by the Incomparable's friend, the Incognita, and that she will not remain many days longer any Unknown."

Elise laughed. "Whoever—I never heard such fustian in all my life! The Incomparable and the Incognita! I ask you!"

Lady Charlotte, however, merely smiled. A lesser lady might have felt the pangs of jealousy at being asked to share her title with another female, but Lady Charlotte, having been brought up from infancy to consider herself a Pearl beyond Price and a Diamond of the First Water, was unable to feel anything but pleased with her friend's cutting a dash in the ton. "To be awarded a soubriquet is the highest degree of fashion," she assured her friend in the gravest tones. "Imagine! The Dark Incognita! Your fortunes are made, my love! You are going to be all the crack!"

Miss Pellerin picked up Fluff from his position

at her hem, where he had been demanding her
attention. Absently, she stroked the silky fur.
"Charlotte, this is very good of you, but I am
not precisely certain that I wish to be all the
crack! If indeed I ever could be, which I do not
think entirely likely— No, my dearest, you must
not look at me so! It is not that I don't appreciate your efforts, for indeed I do, and it is extremely wonderful to be dressed in the height of
style, and to be taken to the opera, but—"

"But nothing, love!" Lady Charlotte inter-
jected. She could not conceive of a female who
would not wish for the lifestyle she had chosen
to lead, and the slightest degree of impatience for
Elise's modesty penetrated her voice. "Elise, you
did not roll your hair last night, and you look as
if you slept askew upon the pillow! From now
on, you must remember to sleep in one position,
and you must, my dear, remember to smoothe
Olympian Dew into your skin every night.
Beauty, as George says, is only maintained at the
price of vigilance!"

Miss Pellerin suppressed a smile and replied
meekly that she would do her best to remember
these strictures. But her face grew serious again.
"Oh, Charlotte, I do so hope that Mr. Woodville
will give Noel serious consideration! It would
mean so much to Uncle and to me if he were
awarded a respectable post where he would be
able to advance his career—"

Lady Charlotte, who held no extremely high

opinion of Noel Pellerin, or more than a hazy conception of Mr. Woodville's power in the Foreign Office, merely smiled and patted her friend's hand reassuringly. "Christian was so attentive to you last night! Indeed, I have never seen him— well, not in absolute *dog's years*—pay so particular an attention to a female! Do you not think him attractive?"

Elise blushed and turned her head away, feigning a great interest in Fluff's ribands. "I have always thought Mr. Woodville to be a most intelligent and interesting person, but I—I was a trifle thrown out of countenance by his attentions last night. He has never paid more than common civility to me before—"

"All the more reason to follow a beauty regime of the most stringency!" Lady Charlotte said decisively. "Besides, my dear, I really do think that there can be nothing happier than having the attention of a gentleman who could influence your brother's future. That Mr. Woodville likes you must affect his attitude toward Noel, you know!"

"Fustian!" Elise protested. "I am sure that Mr. Woodville has much more principle than that! Besides, Charlotte, I think you make too much of a little thing! I think that Mr. Woodville is merely being civil because he finds me a conversant companion with mutual interests in art. He is merely being polite!"

Lady Charlotte concealed her smile behind her chocolate cup.

By the ormolu clock in the library, the hour was just past five when Mr. Woodville was admitted to his own residence by Coe. As he stripped his gloves and handed over his coat to the footman, he glanced at the silver salver on the table, grinning sardonically at the pile of visiting cards.

"Heavy day?" he inquired of his servant.

"Yes, sir, that it has been," the footman confided to his master. "If you'll pardon my saying so, sir, I've been quite run off my feet, opening the door to every rig and swell on the town."

"Ah," Mr. Woodville said. "The ladies about?"

Coe relieved his master of his broad beaver. "Her ladyship's on the strut with Lord Brandamore, sir, and Miss Pellerin is in the library, painting, I believe." He lowered his voice. "In oils, sir," he added in the tones of one who has witnessed a very odd event.

Woodville entered that room shortly thereafter to find Miss Pellerin seated by the bay window, a green baize apron covering her jersey afternoon dress of apricot, ornamented with bands of russet silk. She had tied a cap about her russet curls, but the fading afternoon light, which cast her high profile into sharp relief, made this proclamation of the spinster state seem unnecessary to his eye. Her face was transfixed with a serene concentration, and she was carefully studying the small easel she had set up upon the table before her, sketching at the small canvas with a series of swift sienna strokes. Beside her on the table, she had spread out her paint kit.

"What? A white canvas?" he inquired gently, and she looked up with the expression of someone who has been sharply removed from a dream, her dark eyes seeming to look past him for a single second before an awareness of his presence flooded back into her being; and she smiled at him, almost too carelessly rising and dropping a linen pall over the canvas. "Merely something I learned from M. d'Angelle, who, I believe had it from Billy Turner. A light background, you see, makes it that much easier to configure your *chiaroscuro*."

Woodville was too polite to press her for a view of the started work, attributing her reticence to a very becoming female modesty. "I hope," he added, advancing toward him hesitantly and untying the strings of her apron, "that you will not object to my setting up a studio in your library. Lady Charlotte assured me you would not, and the light is very good in this room—"

"Not at all," Woodville assured her. "I make more use of my study, you know! But I am surprised that you would find time to paint. By the size of that pile of visiting cards, I thought perhaps your time would be taken up with social pursuits!"

Elise smiled. "Indeed, it is the most famous thing! The doorbell has never stopped ringing all this morning, and Charlotte has received invitations to" —she began to tick off upon her fingers as she listed the events— "rout parties, rout balls, which I must remember are different things entirely, assemblies, balls, balls masked, and balls *formal*, parties, musical evenings, concerts of ancient music, dinners, luncheons, showings, Venetian breakfasts, and oh, yes, a balloon ascension!"

"A ballon ascension!" Woodville repeated.

"Oh, Lord Brandamore assures me it is quite fashionable," Elise returned, her eyes twinkling. "Indeed, I have been most gratified to find that Lord Brandamore and Charlotte are determined to make me quite odiously fashionable myself. I feel a bit as if *I* might be a balloon ascension!"

"Or the Dark Incognita!" Mr. Woodville suggested and was rewarded with a look of distress.

"That, I assure you, is none of my doing. Indeed, when Charlotte read that bit from the newspaper to me, I did not know where to look! But Mr. Foxmere assured me this morning that only diamonds of the first water are accorded such titles, and while I may not be a diamond of the first water, it was excessively kind of him to say so!"

"What, Foxmere here?" Mr. Woodville asked, startled. "He ain't one of Charlotte's *cicisbei!*"

"That is what Lord Brandamore told me, too. But he came with his sister, who seemed not to think very much of Charlotte either, and indeed, he spent his whole time talking to me, so I think perhaps he might be shy. After all, Charlotte is so recently out of black gloves that he might feel a bit hesitant to press his suit in her direction."

"Not likely!" he replied. "If I know Charlie, he'd have been sitting in Charlotte's pocket long before this! More likely it's you he's formed a tender for, Miss Pellerin!"

The lady looked faintly startled. "Oh, I doubt that, you know, for he asked both Charlotte and me for a place upon our cards at Almack's! And only after Lord Brandamore had been most particular to ask me to stand up with him! Shall I be dead bored by Almack's? Lord Brandamore says it is very stuffy, but procuring a voucher is an absolute necessity if one wishes to be considered of the highest ton!"

Mr. Woodville's lips twitched. "Oh, the most deadly spectacle in town, I assure you! The Marriage Mart, as you must know by now, is slow-topped, with only orangeat, lemonade and champagne punch being served, and no lady is allowed to dance the waltz without the consent of one of those four patronesses!"

Miss Pellerin nodded. "That is what Sir Francis Garvey tells me. He promised that he would secure me a cachet from Lady Jersey, however, for he intends to be so kind as to attempt to instruct me in the steps of the dance!"

"Fran Garvey?" Woodville asked. "He was here?"

"Is he not a friend of Lady Charlotte's?" Elise asked naively.

Since Lt. Sir Francis Garvey was definitely not renowned for his cultivation of friendships outside of the military set, he could only shake his head. "A passing acquaintance, I believe! Tell me, did Sir Francis also seem to spend a great deal of time in conversation with you?"

Miss Pellerin nodded. "He was nice enough to offer to escort me to Gloucester House any time I wished to go there. He said that his cultural education was sadly lacking, and that he would derive the greatest benefit from my being able to point out which of the pictures he must most admire!" She laughed, shaking her head. "He is very droll, you know, even if he does not appreciate art."

"Who else called this morning?" Mr. Woodville asked, fascinated.

"Oh, now that Charlotte is out of black gloves, a great many people have come past to pay their respects. Lady Sefton was gracious enough to bring my voucher, and so kind as to introduce her nephew Mr. Knightley to me, though Charlotte said he is in the basket and not to be taken seriously, since he is only interested in heiresses, which I assure you, I am not; and there was Colonel Wilcox, he came with Sir Francis, of course, most dashing in those hussar uniforms; and Lord Beckwith; and Mr. Trent; and oh, Lady Arabella Rippon and her brother Mr. Young; and Sir Toby Smudge, who Charlotte says is as rich as a golden ball, though it was acquired in trade; and—" Gaily, Miss Pellerin reeled off a list of names. Although Mr. Woodville was able to discern several of Lady Charlotte's *cicisbei* and suitors among the lot, he was shrewdly able to select the names of several gentlemen, for whom, he accurately guessed, the main attraction of a visit to Upper Mount Street was not Lady Charlotte Woodville, but her dark companion. For some reason, this information made him feel vaguely uneasy, and it was only his excellent manners which allowed him very civilly to congratulate Miss Pellerin upon her conquests.

"My—conquests?" she replied. "Oh, I hardly think so, you know. I am far beyond the age or the inclination to have conquests!" With a single careless gesture, she dismissed some of the most eligible prizes of the Marriage Mart. "But enough of me, Mr. Woodville," she entreated, suddenly serious. "All this day I have been cast into an agony of apprehension equal to any of Charlotte's novel heroines, waiting for news of your decision upon my brother."

The smile upon Mr. Woodville's features stiffened slightly. "Yes, your brother," he said, a trifle less enthusiasm in his voice than Elise might have wished for. "Well, I have accepted him in the position of my foreign secretary—on probation!"

The relief that flooded through Miss Pellerin's face was gratifying to him. Even more so was the light touch of her fingers upon his arm as she strove to thank him in a very pretty manner. "—Thank you, so very much. You have made both my uncle and me so very happy. Noel must be pleased to know that his feet have been firmly set upon his career in the Foreign Service. Thank you so very much."

"Wait, Miss Pellerin, not so fast!" Mr. Woodville warned her gently. "For your sake, and for Comte Pellerin's sake, I have agreed to take Noel on trial, as it were. The position I have offered him is not, I fancy, precisely where he believes his ambitions, if not his talents, lie; but I don't think he's ready for the position of prime minister quite yet!" He tried to soften these words, but Miss Pellerin, whose extreme fondness for her younger brother could almost render her blind to his faults, looked rather distressed.

"He is very young, I know, Mr. Woodville, but patience, you know, is not his virtue, and he is excessively clever, and very good with languages and political science—"

"I am sure that he is, and I hope that he shall have every opportunity to display his talents in the very near future. But the lad kept me cooling my heels for quite a half hour above the agreed time before he made his appearance and, on top of that, told me to my face that he considered any position I might offer him to be quite below his rank as a prince!" He shook his head sadly. "The boy needs a firm hand, Miss Pellerin, but I hope, perhaps in time, when he's acquired a bit of town bronze and some experience in the world, that he will come about. Mind you, I don't promise, but for all of that, he has potential, and I shall see what I can do. I've got him working down translations of dispatches to Spain right now, and if he's turned his hand well at that, I might see about placing him with Sir Horace Lacey's mission to Perisa . . ."

"Oh, Mr. Woodville, you are entirely too good!" Miss Pellerin exclaimed. "I cannot thank you enough. Noel will do his best, I promise!"

It was upon the tip of Mr. Woodville's tongue to remind her that she should not promise what she could not deliver, but instead he smiled down at her radiant face. "If you wish to repay me, Miss Pellerin, you will put off that apron and change into your driving coat. If you wish to add to your consequence, after all, you must be seen driving in the park behind my grays!"

Elise untied the knots of the apron. "Oh, then are you very fashionable?" she teased him.

Mr. Woodville nodded gravely. "*Insupportably* tonnish, and I rarely take up females; so you may be assured that all the world will know exactly how *à la mode* you are! Now, go and get your hat!"

Miss Pellerin was unaccustomed to the pastime of riding in the park at the fashionable hour in a precarious vehicle known as a high-perch phaeton, with its seat suspended above its yellow-rimmed wheels, behind a team of perfectly matched high-steppers. After her initial fear that Mr. Woodville might send them both toppling to the ground as they threaded their way through the promenade at the spanking pace, she began to enjoy herself immensely, seeing and being seen in this tonnish mode.

Mr. Woodville flicked his whip at his leader's ear in a way his tiger, sitting up behind them, considered a bit too toffish, and stole a sideways glance at Miss Pellerin as he threaded their way through a narrow gate with only a few inches to spare on either side.

With her dark curls peering out beneath a very fetching toque of russet velour, ornamented with two short plumes of daffodil, and a chocolate-colored driving coat done in the military style with gold frogs and epaulets, her hands tucked into the warmth of a large sable muff, and little half-boots (of orange jean) upon her feet, she was an ornament that any gentleman would be proud to have beside him, Mr. Woodville thought rather fondly.

As they wheeled down Rotten Row, he pointed out to her such notable sights as Tommy Onslow's phaeton and four; Poodle Bingham with his famous canine up beside him; Lady Ombersley upon her Arabian stallion, quite the most notable horsewoman in the country, and famous for her hunt in the shires; a landaulet containing no less a set of personages than York and Gloucester, two of the more corpulent royal dukes, both of whom signaled Mr. Woodville down and demanded introduction to his companion, proclaiming the greatest interest in Comte Pellerin's niece in such a way that Elise might have been put to the blush had the park been more private and Mr. Woodville not quite so haughty. In the course of the ride, she espied a great many of her new acquaintances from that morning, and Mr. Woodville was several times obliged to pull over so that Miss Pellerin could converse with this person or that upon the saunter, a favor he performed with something less than good nature, which he strove to conceal beneath an impassive demeanor.

When they had come into the open pathway beneath the elms, and there was no sight of anyone who might possibly engage Miss Pellerin's attentions, he brought the phaeton to a halt. "Would you care to take your hand at the ribands?" he asked, causing his tiger to choke at this unprecedented move from his master, who had been known to refuse his reins to even such a whip as the aforementioned Lady Ombersley on the grounds of her sex. No female, he had been known to say, could possibly credit herself with the necessary skills and strength to handle a prime team.

"Coo, guv'nor!" the tiger protested. "Ye ain't 'andin' over no leather to no mort whilst *I* sits h'upon the box!"

He received, for his pains, a quelling look. "Very well, Jerry, than you may step down while I instruct Miss Pellerin! I don't pay you for your opinion, my boy!"

The tiger looked sorely offended at the idea that he would desert his master upon any provocation whatsoever, and Miss Pellerin declared that Jerry showed better sense than his master. This seemed to mollify that young man's pride somewhat, for he stoically crossed his arms across his livery and, looking over their heads, announced that if Miss was truly wishful to be handling leather, he would suggest that she could not be with a better teacher.

Since most of this was delivered in a Cockney so thick as to be almost incomprehensible to Miss Pellerin, she was forced to take the tiger's lofty nod in her direction for his assent to the program, and hesitantly threaded the guides through her gloved fingers.

Jerry was correct—that Mr. Woodville was a good teacher—and it was not long after a series of stops and starts that Miss Pellerin was gently taking the phaeton over one of the less-traveled paths through the Arboretum. Jerry even forgot himself as far as to offer his own terse instructions to her, which Mr. Woodville, with tongue firmly in cheek, was translating for her when she drew up rather abruptly beside a tall gentleman in a checkered waistcoat, strolling along the pathway.

Mr. Woodville murmured something under his breath, but Elise had already leaned down from the perch to allow the man to take her hand into his own. "Emile! Of all things famous!" she exclaimed warmly. "How are you?"

With a flourish and a smile that did not quite reach his eyes, M. Bertraine swept his high-crowned beaver from his carefully pomaded locks, in the same look shrewdly appraising both Elise's costume and her companion. "My dearest Elise," he drawled in French. "How very *anglais* you have become, driving round the park in such a handsome rig—and in such fashionable company," he added.

Elise turned to Mr. Woodville, slightly puzzled by the wooden expression on his countenance. "Mr. Woodville, may I present my friend, M. Bertraine?"

Woodville nodded. "We have met," he said stiffly, looking at Bertraine in an almost fierce manner.

Bertraine's eye met Elise's, and he shrugged almost imperceptibly. Stung by Woodville's apparent rudeness, Elise conveyed her most devastating smile upon her old friend. "I saw you at the opera last night, Emile. Why did you leave before the first act and not even come up and say hello to me?" she chided him gently.

Bertraine shrugged. "I hear your direction is with Lady Charlotte Woodville now, and you are coming into society under her aegis!"

Elise nodded. "I am only staying with her for a small time. You remember her as Charlotte St. Ives, perhaps, when she and I were in school together?"

"Ah," Bertraine said. "And now I remember, of course. How very stupid of me. And this must be Mr. Woodville, who has employed our Noel?"

"Correct," Woodville responded in repressed accents. For a moment, his eyes locked with Bertraine's. "We *have* met before," he said softly.

"You recall. I am so very glad," Emile responded evenly, turning his attention back to Elise. "How very grand you have become my dearest! Doubtless you shall forget all of your old *émigré* friends now that you are moving in the first circles."

"Emile! How could you think such a thing?" Elise demanded. "Of course I do not forget my friends! You must come to call upon Lady Charlotte! I am certain that *she* will be glad to see you," she added with a speaking glance at Mr. Woodville.

Bertraine shrugged. "Perhaps. But I think—well, I shall hope to see you at your uncle's. I have taken Noel under my wing. Our little one is most anxious to take himself upon the town, you know, and someone must protect him from the sharps and flats, eh, Mr. Woodville?"

"Quite so, sir," was the distant reply.

Reluctantly, Elise allowed her hand to be disengaged from Emile's. "You will come to call?" she asked almost defiantly, and he shrugged lazily.

Almost before she could complete her good-byes, Mr. Woodville had removed the ribands from her hand and was engaging the phaeton to move on at a smart pace.

Beside him, Elise's cheeks burned, and she could not bring herself to look at her companion. Decidedly, Mr. Woodville must think himself of great consequence to be so rude to poor Emile, she thought. What would he know of the sufferings Emile had endured? How he had seen every possible path closed off to him by the prejudice of just such powerful men as Mr. Woodville, until the only avenue open to him was the gambler's life? At least he never cheated at cards, or used loaded dice, the way she had heard Emile say so many so-called gentlemen of Mr. Woodville's class were known to do. What would someone like Woodville, whose pockets were never to let, and who had never gone hungry a day in his life, know of Emile's hardships? Easy enough to look down your fine nose *then*, sir! she thought, unconsciously tilting her own chin upward and sitting up very straight in the seat.

"How do you come to know M. Bertraine?" Woodville asked as they entered the row again. Elise glanced at him sharply. Although his tone seemed to be neutral, almost casual, she thought she detected the confirming hauteur beneath the surface.

With a great deal of effort, she forced herself to reply in an equally neutral voice, "All of my life. His family and my own have been allied for many centuries."

"I see." Mr. Woodville replied. With one almost lazy stroke, he flicked at his leader's ear. "I do not think that Charlotte would enjoy his company, you know," he added gently. "Brandamore would tell you that he is not at all tonnish, and nothing could be more uncomfortable than to press Charlotte's good nature into receiving someone she would not like in her own home."

"I understand," Elise replied stiffly, unable to find a suitable retort to a statement that was, alas, perfectly true.

Although Mr. Woodville several times addressed the most leading remarks to Miss Pellerin during the remainder of the drive, she

responded with only the most trivial commonplaces, refusing to rise to his baited wit.

When he finally set her down in front of the
house, she thanked him with cool civility for the
ride and turned to walk up the steps before he
could assay a reply.

As Mr. Woodville watched Basile open and
close the green door for Miss Pellerin, he
whistled absently through his teeth, then hitched
up his leaders for the short drive around to the
mews.

"That Monsoor Bertraine's a cavey flash
cove," Jerry remarked shrewdly.

"That he is," his master replied thoughtfully.
"More so, I fear, than poor Miss Pellerin may be
aware of."

"And 'er bein' so prime to the mark, you'd a
think she'd deep-say 'im as one for the nubbing-
cheat," the tiger observed. "For, aside from Miss
bein' a mort an' all, she do know 'ow to 'andle 'er
cattle—for the furst time h'out, o'course.'"

A rare smile twisted Mr. Woodvilles lips.
"That she does," he agreed. "And she has the
face of a Giotto Madonna, wouldn't you agree?"

Jerry, too young to appreciate female beauty,
allowed as how there were some who might say
she was a prime'un, but he hoped that his master
was not going to be so foolish as to repeat today's incident and allow her to take the leaders
again.

"I hate to disappoint you, my boy," Mr. Woodville said firmly, "but I have every intention of allowing Miss Pellerin to drive as much as she likes! And, Jerry, it will be your duty to be sure that no harm comes to her when I'm not about! Is that understood?"

The tiger, upon whom it was beginning to dawn that his master might be turning a shade dotty in his dotage at twenty-seven years, stared. But his worst fears were allayed.

"And none of your impudence, young'un! I'll thank you to hold your gab and be sure that Miss Pellerin don't spend overmuch time with Bertraine without my knowledge! Even you don't care to see a mort knocked about, do you?"

"Coo!" Jerry breathed.

"Exactly so, Jerry! This time I fear we have taken on a bit more than bargained for with the Pellerin family!" He frowned thoughtfully. "I only hope that our bird will take the bait without plucking us!"

With this cryptic remark, he swung himself easily down from the perch and tossed the leathers to his tiger. "Mind you do what I told you!" he admonished his small employee.

"Course I will!" Jerry replied, gazing upon his master with adoring loyalty only partially disguised by his outward indignation that Mr. Woodville would ever doubt his ability to follow an order, no matter how mysterious.

Mr. Woodville, after all, was a deep cove,

though you wouldn't know it by the fine airs and graces he put on. Over his pictures and his fine manners, he was as tough as steel, and there wasn't much that went past his fly box!

Chapter Six

"There you are, my dear!" Lady Charlotte fluttered from her boudoir when she espied Elise walking past. "Where have you been, you sly puss?"

Elise, caught in the act of trying to pass Charlotte's open door without attracting attention to herself, paused in the doorway. Her eyes were vaguely troubled. "Out driving with Mr. Woodville, of course!"

Lady Charlotte smiled. Having been informed of this most interesting development by Elder when Miss had come for her coat and hat, she felt a definite sense of "doing the right thing," which entitled her to have a certain proprietary interest in developments. "Did you have a very good time with Christian? He is considered to be a most creditable whip, you know, and he never takes up females in that phaeton of his. Well, hardly ever! I myself have rarely been driving with him above two or three times. Of course, he took up Miss Baldistone, but that doesn't signify, for I am convinced she was a wretched flirt, and doubtless she *badgered* him into it!"

Elise drew a deep breath, sorting out these sentences. "Oh, it was well enough. We encountered the royal princes, but Charlotte, they were *amazing!*"

Lady Charlotte giggled in a fashion quite unmatronly. "Oh, yes! They are a couple of quizzes, but wait until you meet Prinny! His corsets *creak!* When my poor Vincent introduced me to him, it was all that I could do to make my curtsy and not go into whoops, which would never have done!"

"I can believe that, if one may judge by his brothers," Elise returned. "York quite stared me out of countenance! I did not know where to look!"

"You mustn't mind them," Lady Charlotte replied airily. "Poor York is quite nearsighted you know. But you will understand if you ever see Mrs. Clarke, for a homelier female would be hard to find, unless of course it were Mrs. Fitz! Poor Prinny. Now that Mr. Brummell is no longer with us, who will restrain the royal brother's excesses?"

"And, of course, Mr. Woodville was so obliging as to allow me to take the ribands," Elise continued. "Though I fear I do not measure up to his tiger's standards."

"What? Oh, Elise, how famous! I do believe Woodville must be most partial to you, for he has never, to my knowledge, allowed *anyone* to take his team, not even my poor Vincent, who, you must know, was considered to be top-o'-the-trees!" Lady Charlotte clapped her hands together, her eyes sparkling. "Do you feel the least partiality toward Christian?"

Elise bit her lip, drawing off her gloves thoughtfully. "He is a most amiable gentleman, of course, but, oh, Charlotte, I did not know that he was a *snob!* Do you recall Emile Bertraine?"

A slight crease appeared upon Lady Charlotte's fine forehead. "Bertraine, Bertraine! No, I do not recall, but one is forever encountering mushrooms with the most encroaching manners. George says the most effective remedy is a set-down, but I can never force myself to be uncivil to anyone! But that is of no consequence my love! Brandamore and I have put our heads together and come up with the most marvelous idea for a very small ball, only a hundred or so couples, and a very small sit-down dinner beforehand, to fire you off after your debut at Almack's. I thought perhaps we could have the Pandean Pipes, and that we could get up the ballroom with a pink silk tent! Would that not be the most marvelous thing?"

Reminding herself firmly that her scatter-brained friend had nothing to do with Mr. Woodville's rude manners, and besides was blessed with a golden heart, Elise merely smiled. "You must do as you like, Charlotte! If you wish to have a ball, do so, but please do not feel that you must have it upon my account!"

"That's what George says! How very pretty your manners are Elise! Of course it shall be a ball for you—and for me, also, to mark the end of my year for poor Vincent. Though," she added, placing a hand against her mantua, "I really feel as if I shall never stop mourning him. It is so hard to go on without someone to advise one as to precisely how things should be done, and it is often very hard for me to *think*. Well, that don't signify, I daresay! I shall manage tolerably well when—if—Christian— Well! Now, tell me who you would wish to invite. Do you have any preferences?"

Elise allowed herself to be drawn into this plan. "Well, my uncle, of course, and Noel, Mr. Foxmere, and Sir Francis. Mr. Beckford should come, I think. Lord and Lady Elgin, they have always been most kind, and we must go and see the marbles before they come, you know! And perhaps Sir George Beaumont, if you don't mind his odd habits. Mr. Turner? Mr. Lawrence? Mr. Turner I do not think would come, but it would be wise to send him an invitation anyway, and the Duc d'Orléans, of course, and yes," she added mischievously, M. Bertraine. He is a most particular friend of my family, you see."

"All these Somerset House people!" Lady Charlotte murmured, scribbling furiously. "We shall be quite overrun with artists, I fear, but perhaps that will persuade Christian that he must be present, for in general he *hates* large parties and only puts in an appearance to be civil. But this time, I daresay that he will stay all night! Shall I make your fortunes and invite the royal dukes?"

"No!" Elise said firmly, then burst into laughter, her gray mood quite forgotten. "Dear Charlotte, what a goose I am! Do forgive me! You do whatever you want, and I promise you I shall try not to disgrace you!" Elise bestowed a quick embrace upon her friend and went off to change for dinner.

"Now whatever did she mean by that?" Lady Charlotte asked of Fluff, lying on his blue satin pillow in the corner of the room.

The small dog answered with a disinterested yawn.

"I daresay you're quite right," Lady Charlotte answered.

If Miss Pellerin was hoping for enlightenment over dinner upon Mr. Woodville's behavior, she was disappointed. The master, Basile informed the ladies, had been suddenly called away on

most pressing business in the Foreign Office, and
was not expected home until quite a late hour.

As Lady Charlotte had engaged herself and
Elise to attend an evening of ancient music at the
residence of two of her most terrifying maiden
aunts, indeed so terrifying that even Lord Brandamore was afraid to deny their summons to
what would surely be a most dreadfully flat evening, the ladies were off quite early, and Elise
had no time to ponder any further upon Mr.
Woodville's behavior.

When she awoke in the morning, she was convinced that it was a small matter and probably
had less to do with snobbery than with some
other emotion in Mr. Woodville's breast. While
she dared not flatter herself that he was jealous,
she hoped that he had noted Mr. Bertraine's interest.

She found herself smiling in a most foolish
manner at her reflection in the mirror, her hair-
brush suspended over her dark head, and
blushed furiously at herself. "Goose! Do not try
to pin your hopes in that direction!" she hissed at
herself, then laid the brush down as it occurred
to her that not even her most repressive common
sense was able to obscure completely the fact
that she was developing a decided partiality for
Mr. Woodville's company.

—But he said you painted like a man, her
common sense said sternly.

—But he was so handsome, and so sure of

himself, and he knew so much about art, Elise dreamily rejoined herself. When I looked up, and he was standing there, I thought he was perfect.

—And he barely noticed you, little mouse, her common sense replied.

—But he notices me now! Elise countered.

—Only because you are in his household. What would he want with an inconsequential little *émigré?* The best you could expect is a carte blanche from Mr. Woodville. Look at the way he treated Emile!

Elise tossed her head, almost defying that much-admired common sense. "We shall see!" she promised, turning away from the mirror.

"—Ah, but have a care, Elise. He can break your heart, her common sense said, having, as usual, the last word.

Fortunately, she had no time to brood over the matter that day, for from the moment she rose from the breakfast table until lunchtime, she was preoccupied with a succession of morning callers.

In the afternoon, Sir Francis escorted Lady Charlotte and Miss Pellerin to Gloucester House for a viewing of the much-discussed Elgin Marbles. While Lady Charlotte and Sir Francis, quickly bored with what that most military gentleman described as "some odds and ends of old marble, not worth half the fuss," debated Lord Elgin's removing them from their place of discovery in Greece against the wishes of Turkish government, Elise yearned for pencil and paper to make sketches of the smooth pinkish stone, admiring the work of the ancient sculptor. Only reluctantly did she allow Sir Francis to persuade her to come away from them to have frozen ices at Mme. Givray's famous cafe in Piccadilly, and only when Lady Charlotte, who secretly thought she would die of boredom if forced to spend another minute standing in the injurious sunlight, promised that Coe might provide her with suitable escort upon another day when she would have all the time she wished to study them.

Sir Francis, she discovered, though darkly handsome and quite dashing, and certainly everything that was considerate and thoughtful when it came to procuring a table in the crowded cafe, was, well, perhaps a trifle dull. He knew nothing of art, and everything of horses, and as she delicately nibbled at the delicious confection of orange water and ice, she was forced to listen very intently to his story of a foxhunt in the Pyrenees to be able to make even the most insipid comments.

But he was so solicitous of her well-being, and so concerned for her comfort that Miss Pellerin thought she would be extremely cold to refuse his invitation to attend a military review at the palace barracks upon the following Saturday, an acceptance which seemed to afford him so much happiness that Lady Charlotte sighed with sympathy.

"He has forty thousand a year," she murmured wickedly to her friend. "And, my dear, those shoulders!"

Miss Pellerin, with a great deal of effort, suppressed her laughter and advised her friend not to make a cake of herself.

But she had to admit that Sir Francis' devotion made it considerably easier for her to face Mr. Woodville that afternoon, particularly since Lady Charlotte was entertaining the most dull of her *cicisbei*, Sir Toby and Lord Warren, both of whom had been friends of her late husband's. When he repeated his invitation to resume her driving lessons, she accepted with alacrity, and they drove into the park on the most agreeable of terms. Mr. Woodville soon handed her the leathers, and in endeavoring to show her at just how precise an angle she must hold her hands, slipped his strong arms over her own in a most gratifying manner, delivering a stern look over his shoulder at his unbelieving tiger.

It was some fifteen minutes before he disengaged his hold over Miss Pellerin's shoulders and allowed her to take free head down an elm-shaded lane. "There, so! I think I may make a whip out of you yet, Miss Pellerin!" he exclaimed. "You shall put Lady Ombersley in the shade!"

Since there seemed in Elise's opinion very

little chance that she would ever cast this lady, or indeed any other female whip, into the shade, she shook her dark curls, concentrating upon keeping her leader in check.

"Ah, but all the most fashionable ladies must at least endeavor to have the appearance of skill," he rejoined. "And what ton exploits did you conduct today?"

"Sir Francis Garvey was kind enough to escort Charlotte and me to view the Elgin Marbles," Elise replied, "and to view a military review Saturday. We went to Mme. Givray's for ices afterward, but I so wished that I had brought a sketchbook to render something of the lines of the marbles. Turner says that they are quite worthy of being studied for form and style."

"Sir Francis, no doubt, thought them very dull stuff! Not quite in his line at all, I am sure. I daresay only the horse's head interested him."

"Sir Francis," Elise said with a great deal more asperity than she realized, "was quite appreciative of the elegance of the sculpture. He was, however, a trifle restive after a half hour or so. He does not, of course, have the sort of— er—artist's eye that would search out detail or form."

"Ah, but I daresay you shall enjoy the military review. Hours upon hours of sitting in the sun on the parade ground, watching the troops march past—oh, I forgot, he is in a hussar unit! You shall see the troops riding past in their uniforms, and the martial music, I believe, is considered quite stirring by some!"

"I am sure that I shall find it quite interesting!" Miss Pellerin replied in repressive tones.

"For your sake, I hope so," Mr. Woodville murmured under his breath.

She threw him a sharp glance, but his expression could have been described as angelic as he leaned across her arm to gently guide the leaders away from the rail.

Elise turned her thoughts back to a matter of more importance to her. "How is Noel doing?" she asked. "I rather thought he might call in Upper Mount Street, but I have not heard a word from him since that night at the opera!"

Mr. Woodville's face became rather impassive. "So far, he does well enough. The other juniors seem to like him well enough. Your brother has a great deal of charm, you know."

Miss Pellerin's fondness for her sibling allowed her to interpret this remark as a compliment upon his progress. "I am so glad! Thank you so much for giving him an opportunity to demonstrate his abilities, sir!"

Mr. Woodville merely shrugged. "It was nothing, I assure you. There's always a need for good fellows, you know. I only wish that Noel could be persuaded to devote more attention to his work and less to his social life. I saw him last night at the Daffy Club, and between you and me, Miss Pellerin, the company he was in was—well, a bit low!"

Miss Pellerin bit her lip. "I see," she said in a low tone. "Was this company perhaps female?"

Mr. Woodville nodded. "Proper high-flyers!"

Elise shrugged. "Noel has a great deal of—charm for females. Oh, you need not mince words with me upon that head. I was obliged more than once to extricate him from the claws of some harpy when he was at Oxford; so I am no stranger to *that*."

Mr. Woodville thoughtfully nodded. He did not doubt Elise's words at all. "But, it is not just the muslin-set of which I speak, ma'am," he suggested gently. "One might also find some objection to his choice of friendships. . . ."

Miss Pellerin raised her brows. "Really," she said cooly.

"Your brother is a trifle green upon some heads," Mr. Woodville continued tactfully. "Mind, I find no objection in a lad's kicking up a lark or two—Lord knows I've done my share of boxing the watch and bailing out the roundhouse in my salad days. It's what young men do, alas, in the process of becoming older! But, he should have a care . . ."

"If, Mr. Woodville, you are speaking of M. Bertraine, I must assure you that Emile is an old and valued friend of my family. People—people in our position, you see, have not always been accustomed to the easy comforts of your life.

When one is obliged to turn one's hand to survival in a foreign country, it—it is not always easy, or simple! Doubtless you may think M. Bertraine is a Captain Sharp, and not at all the thing, but I assure you, he is received in the best places, despite his occupation and his French ancestry!"

Mr. Woodville laughed. If it was meant to be a pleasant sound, it was not received by Elise as such. "Come now, don't bear-garden men, Miss Pellerin! I did not say that M. Bertraine fuzzed his cards or shot his ivories! And, indeed, there are hostesses who are glad to see his face on their steps. But, if you have a concern for your brother, you will place a word in his ear about allowing Bertraine to *cicerone* him on the town. He would not welcome such advice from me, you see, but from his sister, perhaps a word would be enough to allow him to use more caution! Noel's position places him in the more important realms of Foreign Office business, you see, and—"

"I believe I do," Miss Pellerin interrupted coldly. "And you need say no more upon that head, sir. I have known M. Bertraine for many years, and what you suggest reeks of the worst sort of snobbery. But of course such a distinguished person as yourself would naturally wish to warn my brother away from an influence which could not add to his consequence."

"No, I think perhaps I ought to say more upon this, Miss Pellerin, since you do not seem to—"

"Please, let us say no more upon it," Elise said, torn between the feeling that Mr. Woodville only spoke a pragmatic truth, and a strong suspicion that he was exercising a sort of dreadful prejudice that she had not hithertofore divined in his character.

They rode along in silence for several minutes before her companion, in the most unexpectedly civil manner, sought to divert her from her mood with an amusing anecdote about a recent visit to the studio of Mr. Constable, where he had found that most interesting of modern artists in the act of mixing his pigments with stale beer. This turned into a concerned speculation by his two well-wishers upon the unhappy state of his romantic affairs, and the loyal character of Miss Bicknell, in such sharp contrast to the rather unbending views of her family.

Mr. Woodville was such an ardent supporter of Constable, and so enthusiastic of his rather radical experiments with art, that Miss Pellerin was rather reluctantly turned back into some state of charity with him again.

But this happy state was not totally free of certain doubts, for Miss Pellerin was quite puzzled that a gentleman who could ally himself with those who supported the humbly born Constable's engagement to Miss Bicknell over those who sided with her unexceptionally respectable family's opposition could, with a *volte-face* en-

tirely inconsistent, express a snobbish dislike of
association with Emile Bertraine, whose birth,
though French, was of the bluest blood.

Inconsistency, Miss Pellerin's common sense
told her, was not a quality to be sought out in a
gentleman one professed certain feelings toward;
indeed, any woman of sense must immediately
reject one who displayed such behavior as too
volatile and capricious. Unfortunately, Miss Pellerin found that such enigmatic behavior only increased the initial fascination, for what female
can resist a certain tenderness for the small faults
of a man she is interested in?

"Shall I have a dance with you tonight at Almack's?" Mr. Woodville's voice quite cut across
her thoughts, and she started a bit, realizing that
they had come out of the park and were now in
Upper Mount Street, before the front door. "Or
have your suitors filled your entire card?" Mr.
Woodville demanded with such a good humored
grin that Elise found herself unable to restrain
her own smile.

"Oh, I am not so fashionable yet!" she
promised him, dismounting from the phaeton. "I
seem to have a boulanger open for you!"

"Wretch! I was hoping for the cotillion!" Mr.
Woodville replied. "But I suppose I have been
cut out by Sir Toby—or any one of a number of
fashionable gentlemen!"

Instead of returning his light banter, Miss Pellerin found herself possessed of a desire to inform him that it simply was not so; but before she could reply, he had whipped up his horses again and was headed for the stables.

Chapter Seven

Lord Brandamore paused before the full-length mirrors in the foyer to examine his evening dress, humming along with the strains of the waltz to be heard issuing from the inner portals of Almack's. Delicately, he touched his snowy cravat, done up in his own original style, and satisfied himself that a pair of well-shaped legs in satin breeches, striped silk stockings and black pumps, together with an elegantly cut coat of black bath superfine that showed off his shoulders to advantage, worn with a white silk waistcoat of the most exquisite cut of Weston's art, from which depended a silver watch chain and a single diamond fob—all came *ensemble* to make him the most elegant man present. Only when he had satisfied himself that a fifteen-minute ride in a closed carriage had not lessened his sartorial presence did he turn to cast a critically appraising eye over his two female companions.

Lady Charlotte, her stunning blond beauty complemented by an evening dress of pale blue crepe highlighted with delicate points of silver lace about her decolletage and sleeves, a simple cord of silver bound through her elaborately knotted hair, and an ivory fan carried in one hand, gave her demitrain a gentle kick as she made certain adjustments to the silver net mantilla thrown carelessly over her shoulders, and bit her lips to increase their rosy color.

Behind her, Elise rather shyly allowed herself to be divested of an evening cloak by a maid, and stepped beneath the crystal chandelier to reveal herself fetchingly begowned in Cypress silk embroidered all over with a network of exotic flowers. Her dark hair had been piled, under Miss Elder's capable hands, into a riot of curls which fell about her face in a most becoming manner. In one hand she held a fan made of ivory, painted with delicate cameos, given to her from the hand of her preceptress, Miss Kauffmann. Only a single strand of pearls was knotted about her throat, and her eyes glimmered with excitement.

Brandamore nodded his approval of both of his female companions, stepping aside to allow them entrance into the dancing rooms. For a single moment, he paused in the doorway, regarding with satisfaction the eyes which followed Miss Pellerin's entrance under Lady Charlotte's aegis; then they were both swept away in the press of elegantly garbed dancers.

"So, dear George," said a silky voice beside him, "is that the chit you mean to bring into fashion?"

Brandamore turned to see Lady Jersey smiling up at him, her dancing eyes betraying her most mischievous mood. He relaxed lazily, giving her one of his half-smiles. "Charl's friend, you know. Only right to give her the push!"

"So, that is the Dark Incognita! They are a contrast, you know, and quite lovely! If not for Jersey, I think I should be quite, quite jealous!"

"No one can take the shine off you, Sally old girl," Brandamore replied gallantly. "No one ever could, even when you were a schoolgirl."

The lady known as Silence fluttered. "If I believed a word of that fustian, George St. Ives, I would not be where I am today! Still, she is quite a taking thing, not at all in the ordinary style. French, someone told me?"

"Auguste Pellerin's niece."

"Ah," Lady Jersey nodded understandingly. "She's a princess, you know, though they don't use the title anymore. Her father was Prince d'Angelle; they had quite an estate in Lorraine, I believe."

"Trust you to know all the latest *on-dits*,"

Brandamore said comfortably. "I must admit I didn't know that one myself. Charl's got some bee in her bonnet about bringin' her into the fashion, for some reason. I'm just adding to her cachet."

"How very unlike you!" Lady Jersey replied with a little laugh. "Dear George, I have never known you to place yourself the tiniest bit out of the way for anyone *except* Charlotte! But I thought that even you might draw the line at this! Is she very clever?"

"If you like 'em bookish, she is. But she's good to Charl', and that's what counts, y'know. Dashed odd, bringin' a female into fashion. I shall have to dance with her once or twice, which is a great bore, since I ain't in general a dancing man, but that should knock it out flat!"

"Oh, dear," Lady Jersey giggled despite herself. "George, you are hopeless. When are you going to *understand* what all the world knows and do the right thing?"

"Say, what?" Lord Brandamore blinked at his old friend. "Always do the right thing! Tell me this waistcoat ain't goin' to be all the great go within a week!"

For his pains, Lady Jersey rapped his hand lightly with her fan. "George, how can you be so obtuse?" she demanded, laughing. "Dear, dear, dear! If she is to be all the rage, I think perhaps you ought to introduce her to me . . . if we can possibly tear her away from that crowd of beaus!

The girl seems to be following in Charlotte's steps when it comes to setting up her *cicisbei!* Sir Francis, and Mr. Foxmere—and Lord Torrance! Dear me! Has she a portion?"

"I daresay her uncle will settle on her quite handsomely—he's a warm man, you know, full of juice! But she does have a brother to be settled, also—young fellow attached to Woodville's staff at the Foreign Office."

Lady Jersey digested this information, nodding. Apparently, she made up her mind to Miss Pellerin's advantage, for she tucked her arm into Lord Brandamore's. "Come and escort me over to Charlotte! I have not seen her since Vincent's passing. . . . I shall press her to make your Dark Incognita known to me before they are both snatched up for the dance."

With only three names on her card, Miss Pellerin had rather expected to spend the evening in one of the spindly blue and gilt chairs lined up against the walls for the convenience of chaperones, while Lady Charlotte danced with her various *cicisbei* and suitors. After all, the reemergence of such a young and beautiful widow as her friend was more than likely to cause quite a stir among the gentlemen present.

It was therefore with a great deal of pleased surprise that Elise found, after Lord Brandamore had very politely stood up with her for the cotillion, and Lady Charlotte had introduced her to Lady Jersey, that a very gratifying number of gentlemen sought out her hand, and vied among themselves as to whom should fetch her a glass of lemonade or pick up her fan, or hold her shawl or escort her to the footholds of balconies for a breath of fresh air when the room became odiously stuffy. How many times she danced, and with whom, she did not know, and when she was obliged to sit out the waltzes, there always seemed to be one or two gentlemen who found pressing reasons not to perform this dance. Nonetheless, she was gratified to watch Lady Charlotte spinning about the floor with Lord Brandamore, and for the first time it suddenly occurred to her that she was not so wholly given over to her own selfish pleasures as to fail to notice what a remarkably handsome pair they made. A tiny smile played about her lips, and when the Honorable Mr. Russell politely inquired what she had found that amused her so, she was forced to reply with the most trivial commonplaces.

At precisely two minutes before eleven, an almost unknown figure appeared upon the threshold, attired in the first mode of elegance. As he handed over his hat and coat to the elderly majordomo, he might have been expected to be gratified by that person's respectful remarks. "Mr. Woodville, sir! We have not seen you here in many, many years! It is indeed an honor, if I may say so, sir!"

Before Woodville could reply, Sally Jersey's

sharp eye had detected his entrance, and she approached him with her fluttery, graceful stride, holding out her hand. "Christian! How do you go on? Whatever brings you here? Has Southbey's closed its doors forever?"

Woodville laughed lightly. "Hardly, Sally," he replied, with a rather droll look of great pain. "Can't I even thrust my head in the door without causin' you to come down upon me?"

She shook her head at him. "Not when we have such need of gentlemen as elegant as you here! No, nothing less will do than an immediate explanation of your presence!"

"Ah, Sally, don't come the bear garden with me, if you please! You know with Boney sprawling across Europe I haven't had a moment's peace in months—" His voice trailed away as he scanned the dancers, frowning slightly. "I thought," he continued lightly, "that Charlotte might be here tonight. That damned George usually drags her into your Marriage Mart!"

Had these remarks been made by anyone else but Mr. Woodville, Lady Jersey would have been forced to administer a most blistering set-down. But since she had formed one of her tendres for him, she merely laughed. "Really Christian! It does you no good to speak of the most fashionable man in London in that manner! Indeed, you should quake in your boots to incur George's displeasure! We all do, you know, for he sets the tones!"

Mr. Woodville shrugged. "Coxcomb!" he remarked impatiently, his eyes flickering across the dancers on the floor. "Ah, there's Charlotte, dancin' with Hyde-Walters! But where's—"

"The Dark Incognita!" Lady Jersey exclaimed, understandingly. "I see what's drawn us to you! She is not at all precisely *light,* is she? But she is very droll and full of humor; so I am quite forced to like her, despite her intelligence!"

"And yet, you do not give her permission to waltz, I see," Brandamore continued.

"She is *Maria's* protégé," Lady Jersey countered, then shrugged, laughing. "I see! Well, then come with me, Christian, and I shall give her her cachet to waltz! But only for your sake, mind you, you wicked man!"

"Sally, you are the veriest angel!" Woodville replied.

"And you, the devil himself!" she laughed.

Elise, who had been sipping her lemonade and listening to Lt. Sir Francis Garvey's account of a very long horse-dealing episode he had encountered at Tattersall's, was surprised when she looked up into Lady Jersey's piquant face. "You do not dance, Miss Pellerin," that lady said. "Would you allow me to introduce you to a suitable partner? Miss Pellerin, Mr. Woodville . . ."

"I shall owe you a debt, Sally," Mr. Woodville murmured under his breath.

"And, old friend, someday I just may collect!" Lady Jersey murmured, smiling at Elise and sweeping away.

Mr. Woodville grinned in a most disconcerting fashion at his rival, Sir Francis, and gave Miss Pellerin a sweeping bow. "May I have this dance?" he asked, taking her hand into his own.

Elise could only nod as she was swept out of her chair and into a pair of powerful arms. Mr. Woodville, who had adorned various embassies of Europe, was an excellent dancer, gently but firmly guiding her hesitant steps through the dance with unexpected elegance and style. As they danced, she was aware of his hooded eyes looking down at her, the corners of his lips slightly lifted in a provoking smile, his arm lightly about her waist, her hand nestled inside of his as they swirled around and around the room, through the other dancers, as if they trod not upon the mundane floors of Almack's, but upon some airy cloud. It was almost a beautiful dream, and she wished that it would never end. This, she thought, this must be how Cinderella felt . . .

All too soon the music ended. They applauded the orchestra without taking their eyes from one another, both of them smiling.

"Are you quite fashionable, Miss Pellerin?" Woodville asked, his eyes twinkling.

"Oh, I think so!" Elise replied. "Thank you very much . . ."

Unfortunately, Mr. Foxmere chose that moment to remind Miss Pellerin that she had promised to make up a set for the country dance next upon the program, and when she turned back to Mr. Woodville, he was gone.

"I say, Charl'," Lord Brandamore drawled in Lady Charlotte's ear, "ain't that Christian? Haven't seen him in Almack's for lo, these many years!"

"Not since Miss Baldistone!" her ladyship replied, a faint smile flickering over her features. "Oh, George, this is famous above all things! I do believe that Christian is forming a decided partiality for Elise!"

"But will he come up to scratch?" Lord Brandamore murmured, swirling his partner down the room. "That's what they'll be laying odds upon in the clubs—and I shouldn't like to lay my blunt on his doing so! Ain't a marryin' man!"

"We shall see," Lady Charlotte murmured, refusing to be daunted. "If they can continue to be brought together in such harmony, he might be persuaded that she would suit him! One only has to look at her to know that she, at least, seems certain of the direction in which her heart lies!"

If Elise had known that her feelings were so obviously betrayed, even to so close a bosom-beau as Lady Charlotte, she would have been quite embarrassed, and indeed, would have vehemently denied the facts. She was much too well brought up to believe that betraying a decided partiality for a gentleman could be anything but the gravest social error. In her private thoughts, nothing could have been more disadvantageous than to mistake Mr. Woodville's attentions for those of a serious suitor. She was a guest in his household, and it behooved him to extend a certain politeness toward her. No doubt he could find in her certain interests similar to his own, and no doubt he enjoyed her companionship; but he had been, she thought, too long upon the town not to be aware that his own consequence would demand that his bride be much more than a simple Miss Pellerin, an *émigré* of an extinct title, the niece of Mr. Woodville's dealer.

Indeed, so narrow was her own estimation of herself that Elise would never perceive that her own feelings were not only reciprocated by Mr. Woodville, but also somewhat in doubt.

When a gentleman has found, to his own disillusionment, that his fortune and consequence have been more highly prized by the ladies of his acquaintance than his person, it is something of a shock for him to discover that he has formed a liking for a female who shares certain of his interests, and that with the course of time, his fondness has turned to love of a far deeper aspect than he has previously experienced. This may be particularly painful when that gentleman is unsure of the lady's feelings toward himself. Certainly Miss Pellerin expressed an agreeable pleasure to be in his company; but she also showed the same pleasure in the company of such cubs as Mr. Foxmere and Sir Francis—not to mention M. Bertraine, who Mr. Woodville had reason to mistrust, reason which concerned certain delicate matters within the scope of the Foreign Office.

Jealousy was an emotion that Mr. Woodville was unaccustomed to experiencing, and it said a great deal for his diplomatic skills that he had striven to conceal this most unbecoming emotion. That the matter was further complicated by his rather exasperating relationship with Mr. Noel Pellerin, as well as his friendship with M. le Comte, made him resolve to put off a declaration until he had found some way of unraveling certain tangled knots of which none of the Pellerins were aware. Both Noel and Elise Pellerin, he had ruefully discovered, could be led but not driven, but he reposed a great deal of hope that he could bring the situation to some resolve without destroying her regard for him. It was the devil's own knot, for he found himself placed in a position where he could not press her with anything but the most casual civility, and must watch, seething with that very uncomfortable newborn emotion of envy, while a court of admirers almost equal to Lady Charlotte's vied for the attentions of the Dark Incognita.

Toward Sir Francis Garvey and Charlie Foxmere he had never felt anything but the ties of good fellowship, until they had started to dangle after Miss Pellerin in what he could only characterize as a moon-calf manner, and if he had been able to land a facer upon the person of Lord Torrance at Jackson's Boxing Saloon with more force than was really necessary in a sparring match, the cause might have been attributed to Lord Torrance's escorting Miss Pellerin to not only a balloon ascension, but a supper party at the Piazza. The duke of York's age, not his exalted rank, spared him from a bruising set-down in the park when he was so kind as to distinguish Miss Pellerin by a few minutes of conversation one day, and even Lord Brandamore, who accepted Christian's usual censures with a certain degree of mildness, was forced to protest most strenuously when Christian seemed ready to offer him physical violence for escorting Lady Charlotte and Miss Pellerin to a very disreputable, if highly fashionable, masked ball at Covent Garden without his consent to the expedition. It was fortunate that only snippets of this last altercation reached Lady Charlotte and Miss Pellerin, or both ladies would have been forced to conclude that Mr. Woodville was in serious danger of losing his senses.

Nothing could be friendlier, or less encroaching than the manner in which he continued to serve Miss Pellerin with her driving lessons, to offhandedly offer to escort her to such attractions as exhibits at the Royal Academy, auctions at Southbey's, visits to the rather amazing Fonthill Abbey, and other such offerings as might be put in the way of one of the prime patrons of the London art world. His behavior was always most civil, and while he was certainly attentive to Miss Pellerin, there was never the slightest hint in his conduct that he was doing any more than enjoying the company of a female with an interest in fine painting.

It was not altogether an unpleasant situation, for Miss Pellerin was content to enjoy Mr. Woodville's company in whatever form he chose to present himself. And if her dreadful common sense sought ruthlessly to suppress any desire to be in his company lest she seriously impair her own hopeless heart, some imp of perversity impelled her to continue to accept his invitations, to derive a certain painful pleasure from the mere presence of the man. The fact that other gentlemen so avidly sought her company eased this pain ever so slightly, but twice she gently steered Sir Francis away from making his proposal that he speak to her uncle, and still, he persisted. Sir Francis was a great believer in the persistence theory in military tactics.

Lady Charlotte could only watch this little dance from a discreet distance, uncertain of what developments were real and what hopes she might cherish were false. Any effort to draw out Elise on her feelings was gently turned aside. Mr. Woodville was all that was polite and consider-

ate, Elise would say gently, her deft fingers
sketching out Lady Charlotte's exquisite face in
pen and ink upon Indian paper; and certainly,
she continued tonelessly, her brow wrinkled with
concentration, one must feel fortunate to count
upon his friendship, and would Lady Charlotte
please sit still?

"I cannot fathom what goes on between them!
It is clear that Christian has developed a decided
partiality for Elise, and she for him, but it is the
most exasperating situation!" her ladyship complained to Lord Brandamore.

This elegant gentleman raised his quizzing
glass and stared at his cousin in disapproval.
"Then, dear Charl', I sincerely advise you not to
try! If you start to meddle, gal—" Faced with
that opaque blue stare, he allowed the glass to
drop on the ribbon. "Well, dash it, bad ton, my
girl!"

Elise's dreadful common sense, a monster
which might sternly suppress any foolish entertainment of strong emotions upon the subject of
Mr. Woodville, also pushed her to have some
anxiety toward her brother. He had been less
than dutiful in calling in Upper Mount Street to
see his sister, and upon the few times she had encountered him at various entertainments, his talk
had been entirely centered about the pleasures to
be found about the town under the patronage of
Emile Bertraine; and by the way, he was a slight
bit beneath the hatches, could she possibly lend

him a tenner until quarter day? That was a good
sister, and he would certainly call soon. Any in-
quiry as to his relationship with his superior, Mr.
Woodville, merely produced a sulky frown and
the muttered observation that Woodville was too
dashed a high stickler for tastes, and what was
the matter of cutting a lark anyway? Such sentiments were not guaranteed to fill his concerned
sister with happiness, but she was fond enough of
Noel to find excuses for his conduct. There must
be much for a young buck on the town to do and
see, and visiting a sister must be dreadfully stuffy
business when compared to the delights of
Covent Garden, Astley's Amphitheater, Spittal-
field's, and any number of other fashionable pursuits that she was certain never came to the ears
of a lady, even a sister most indulgent.

Elise was, however, a dutiful niece who called
frequently upon her uncle in Half Moon Street
and at the gallery. M. le Comte, very much involved in the high season, was engaged in a delicate transfer of a series of Leonardo sketches
from an impoverished peer to a culture-hungry
cit, and could only throw up his hands upon any
questions about Noel. To have a nephew safely
tucked away at Oxford, and to have that same
nephew stumbling into one's well-regulated
household at all hours of the day and night were
apparently two very different things. "I love my
boy!" M. le Comte told his niece, throwing up
his hands. "*Le bon dieu,* He knows that I love

Noel, but under my roof, I will not have *le jeune homme* with his—what do you say?—larks upon the town. To have the constable bringing him home, boxing the watch, is more than I can bear! So, when he tells me that he is taking chambers in St. James Street with Emile, I say *bien entendu,* Emile will keep an eye upon him! So, no more do I see him unless he wishes me to pay his gaming debts!" M. le Comte allowed himself to chuckle indulgently. "This, perhaps he will outgrow, but if this is what is done by the fashionable swells, then I have no objection! He will learn!"

With this pronouncement, Elise was forced to agree, for not all of her experiences in Oxford had quite illuminated for her the perils attendant upon a young man's acquisition of that elusive and highly desirable quality known as town bronze.

If Noel's conduct troubled his uncle only slightly, M. le Comte's niece was proving to present him with a difficulty as taxing to resolve. At first, she was adamant. Not reason, not logic, not an appeal to the damaged state of his nerves could change her resolution to exhibit her painting under a pseudonym. She was impervious to threats to cancel the exhibition altogether, for she knew that her work would be salable, and threaten as he might, her dear uncle was far too shrewd to refuse to show a salable artist. Only by prevailing upon her former preceptress, Maria

Cosway, to show Miss Pellerin to rights, did Comte Pellerin finally prevail.

The delicate widow, on one of her infrequent visits to England, paid a call in Upper Mount Street and, after answering a pelter of questions about her life in Italy and Switzerland, and the success to be found by artists on the Continent, gently turned the conversation around to her erstwhile pupil's work. She was so full of glowing praise for Elise's landscapes, and so interested in her opinions about all that she had seen in London, that it was not too long before Elise was pouring her confidences into Mrs. Cosway's ears. "So, you can see that I *must* exhibit under a pseudonym, Maria! The detractors of female painters—"

Mrs. Cosway shook her head. "No, my dear, you must think of what dear Angelica would have said! She would have advised you to hold your head up! Miss Kauffmann, after all, never cried craven. Nor, I might add, have I, though there were times when I was strongly tempted to do so. True talent, my dear Elise, does not recognize sex!"

By these means and persuasions she was able to bring Elise around to her way of thinking, and they were enjoying a comfortable coze when Mr. Woodville happened upon them.

He was delighted to make Mrs. Cosway's acquaintance, and even more delighted to be able to show her his own collections, taking her through his salons and discoursing with her upon most comfortable terms about the Continent and various mutual friends.

By the end of the afternoon, when Mrs. Cosway took her leave, she was able to satisfy herself that she had not only convinced Elise to exhibit under her own name, but that she would also receive a most interesting announcement about her pupil before too much more time elapsed. A little smile played about her lips as she mounted the steps of her carriage.

"Talking secrets with Mrs. Cosway?" Mr. Woodville teased his companion as they clipped about the park.

Elise looped the rein, nodding, her eyes on the road. "She has convinced me that I must exhibit under my own name. My uncle has been kind enough to—offer me the small gallery for a showing of my canvases, but I thought perhaps that it would not do to—to put myself forward under my own name. People might say that I painted very well for a woman!"

"I wonder who might have said that!" Mr. Woodville remarked.

Elise shot him a sharp glance from beneath her lashes, but his lips were twitching. "Wretch!" she exclaimed. "YOU said that, if you do not recall!"

"I must have been quite, quite mad!" Mr. Woodville said lightly. "You paint most admi-

rably, ma'am. Indeed, I have long wished to tell
you so, but your uncle feared that you would be
mad as fire if you knew that he had shown me
your landscapes before the show."

The look Miss Pellerin chose to bestow upon
him was speaking. "You are odious!" she
laughed; then in a more serious voice, she asked,
"Do you really think so? That I—that the canvases are good?"

"Most excellent," he assured her gravely.
"And I think that you should show them under
your own name, if only to put such cads as I to
the blush of retracting their words!"

Lady Charlotte was no stranger to the planning of entertainments of every variety, from the
Venetian breakfast to the late supper. To receive
one of her engraved cards, headed in Lustre
script, *Lady Charlotte Woodville Requests the
Honor*, was to receive a mark of the highest ton.
When two hundred such cards went out, there
were very few refusals.

With the ease of one who has been accustomed to ordering such things, Lady Charlotte
occupied herself with such chores as the dinner
menu of three courses and thirty removes, along
with the selection of more than seventeen wines,
the engagement and selection of the orchestras,
the procuring of refreshments and champagne
from Gunter's, the procurement of some four
hundred thousand roses to match her pink silk

tents (this last most difficult since roses were decidedly out of season and must be fetched from
the succession houses at Woodville Place), the
directing of linkboys and the notification of the
constables to take care of the traffic a large party
would cause in Upper Mount Street, and a
hundred other small chores. Lord Brandamore
was periodically summoned forth to give his
opinion on this or that point of taste and style, or
to handle some rather specific errand. It might
have been expected, Elise thought, that his lordship would take these matters as quite below his
dignity as a leading light, but he performed his
part with such good grace that she was quite as-
tounded.

For herself, Lady Charlotte kept her quite
busy with a thousand small chores, which Elise
was able to perform in good spirit, and she felt
as if she were learning quite as much about eti-
quette and planning as she would ever need to
know. It was rather like watching a play going
through rehearsals, Elise thought as she ran to
the housekeeper's room for the sixth time in one
day. And though the entire household was in tu-
mult by the day before the affair, Lady Charlotte
remained, like the eye of a hurricane, calm and
cool, even when the draper delivered exactly the
wrong color of silk and Basile threatened to give
his notice if the temperamental individual in the
kitchen did not immediately desist from throwing
cooking utensils at his underlings.

And like a play, it seemed that it would never pull itself together for a performance. Or at least it appeared that way to Elise, when the day of the ball dawned with the sounds of Miss Elder loftily informing Lady Charlotte that since there might be females who dampened their muslins, she was not to say, but such persons were not ladies in her charge, and not at all what Lady Charlotte's dear departed mother or husband would have wished for their own.

Since only the arrival, upon supplication in that quarter, of a very sharp note from Lord Brandamore to the effect that dampening one's muslins was in dashed bad taste won that argument in Miss Elder's favor, Elise hoped that peace would reign for the remainder of the day.

If that rare state did in fact assume charge of the household, she was not aware of it, for she was kept busy with so many last-minute preparations and supervisions that by four o'clock, when Lady Charlotte suggested they both might use a few hours' rest from their labors in order to be fully energized for the evening, she was glad enough to take herself off to her room and repose upon the chaise lounge with a novel. Barely had she scanned the first page before she was drifting off into a comfortable slumber.

Mr. Woodville arrived upon the scene at five, just as two burly workmen in shirt sleeves were setting up an awning across the portico. Coe and the second footman, in baize aprons, were in the process of unrolling the carpet down the marble steps, while Basile, at the top of the stairs, was torn between directing this activity and conferring with the housekeeper over a pile of damask napkins.

"Quite a fete!" Mr. Woodville said, being nearly jostled aside by a housemaid bearing an enormous bouquet of pink roses in the direction of the hall table. Several unopened florist cases reposed most interestingly there also, testifying to the fact that both ladies had received more than their fair share of corsages.

"Yes, sir!" Basile replied, handing Mr. Woodville his mail and relieving him of his hat and coat. "We have had one hundred and ninety-three acceptances so far. Dinner, sir, will be served at eight o'clock, for twenty." He sighed, contemplating a delivery boy easing a cart down into the servant's entry. "It will be a very small gathering compared to what we had in your late father's day, sir, but I feel that it will serve to bring our Lady Charlotte back into the foreground of hostesses, if I may make so bold!"

"Undoubtedly!" said Mr. Woodville dryly. He glanced through the letters in his hand and strolled up the stairs to his own chambers.

He descended the stairs attired in his evening dress a little past eight to find the ladies in the green salon entertaining the first of the dinner guests, Comte Pellerin, resplendent in his evening dress with the *Médaille Louis* and several lesser honors pinned upon his chest.

Lady Charlotte was at her most palely beautiful in a ball gown of chiffon teale over a slip of white satin. It had tiny capped sleeves of lace and silver lustering, and was lavishly trimmed in silver gossamer. The famous Woodville pearls hung from her ears and were looped about her throat. Miss Elder had curled and pomaded her pale blond curls until they shone in the candlelight, bound up above her head with a riband of seed pearls and lamé. A chicken-skin fan painted with scenes from *Bacchante* and tiny silver slippers completed this striking toilette.

Miss Pellerin, in contrast to her friend's blondness, wore a crepe ball-dress of pale pomona green silk, with an overskirt of spider gauze which glimmered in the light as she moved. Her short, tight sleeves were embroidered with delicate fern leaves; and down the front of the dress, the overskirt was parted with figures in this same embroidery. She carried a small gold fan over one gloved arm and wore a thin pomona green shawl across her arms. Her dark hair was dressed in curls *à la méduse,* and as she turned to greet Lord Brandamore, Mr. Woodville's eyes caught hers with the smallest of appreciative smiles.

Even as Mr. Woodville chatted amiably with the arriving dinner guests, charming Lady Jersey with the latest *on-dits,* he kept a portion of his attention upon the doorway, where Basile was announcing the arrivals.

When Noel Pellerin entered the room, greeting his hostess and moving away with his sister, regaling her with some careless tale about a horse that had run lame at Newmarket, Mr. Woodville's eyes narrowed.

Although the young man was dressed with elegance, and his handsome form betrayed no anxiety, there was a certain wariness in the way with which he seemed to be avoiding any greeting to his host, and the laugh which trailed over the conversations in the room seemed to Mr. Woodville to be strained and even a trifle hysterical.

But it was a matter of some delicacy to extricate himself from conversation with Lady Jersey, and just when Mr. Woodville thought he had seen his chance, Basile announced that dinner was served, and there was nothing for it but to offer Sally his arm and escort her into the dining room.

Here, of course, there was no possibility of a conversation with Noel, and Mr. Woodville properly kept his attention upon Lady Jersey on his right and the Countess Maiven on his left. But as the light sole with an anchovy paste was being removed to make way for a *rognon de boeuf*, Mr. Woodville glanced up to see that Noel's plates were going away barely touched, and the footman was pouring him more wine.

". . . Silliest thing to be taxing her head with!

I told her that Rondell was the father of the last Younge brat . . ." Lady Jersey was saying.

At that moment, Mr. Woodville happened, as any good host would, to glance down the length of the table. Lady Charlotte was engaged in earnest conversation with Mr. Foxmere. Comte Pellerin was flirting in a most genteel fashion with Lady Ancille. If Miss Pellerin was in her brother's confidence, she was a better actress than he had reason to suppose she would be, for she was laughing with delight at some chance remark of Lord Jersey's. Noel was seated between Miss Develin and Lady Kershowe, but he was speaking to neither, but staring straight at Mr. Woodville.

It was the look of a condemned man. Noel's face was ghastly pale, until his dark eyes seemed like the sockets of a skull. His lower jaw hung down slightly, exposing a row of white even teeth. For one second, Mr. Woodville thought that he saw the fear in Noel's face, the fear of a trapped rabbit, and then suddenly the look passed as swiftly as it had come. With a gesture meant to convey bravado and irony, Noel raised his wineglass toward Mr. Woodville. But the hand that held it was white-knuckled and trembling, and the boy turned his head away to the superior claims of Lady Kershowe, who was obviously charmed by his youth and beauty.

Mr. Woodville heard himself making the proper reply to Lady Jersey's speculations about the latest gossip, but his mind was working. True, there was no great love lost between himself and his underling. Frequently, he had come down upon Noel for paying more attention to the pleasures of the fashionable life than to applying himself to the business of the Foreign Office, and Noel, cosseted and spoiled all his life by his indulgent uncle and sister, had chafed against authority, particularly when that authority was represented by a gentleman of obvious Corinthian tastes and style, the sort of image to which Noel aspired so desperately.

In general, Mr. Woodville knew that the gentlemen who worked beneath him regarded him as a great-go. He was not so immodest as to believe, despite certain very strong appearances to the contrary, that he was idolized by his underlings, but he had the satisfaction of knowing that he was not considered to be an ogre, like Lord Amherst, or a slave driver, like Mr. Pitt. He was not unfond of Noel, despite the boy's rebellious streak, and was in fact deeply appreciative of the force it must have taken the young man to break away from his uncle and sister. Noel was capable of working well, when he chose, and completing his reports with accuracy and precision. He had never betrayed the slightest reason to be mistrusted with the handling of confidential documents until . . .

But this matter indicated something entirely different. The suspicions which had been forming

in Mr. Woodville's mind since he had received
the anguished communication from his secretary
upon arrival home seemed to be bearing some
fruit. What happened and why, Mr. Woodville
intended to find out before the evening was finished. The document in question was only a
memorandum, yet in the wrong hands, it could
affect the fate of a thousand men. One of Napoleon's spies would be more than willing to pay a
great deal for that little slip of paper, and no
questions asked about how it was obtained.
Enough to pay off gaming debts that must be, if
Mr. Woodville was any judge, pressing indeed.
Even Noel must know, he thought, that a man
may allow his tailor and the rest of his creditors
to dangle, but gaming debts were to be paid off
as soon as possible. And in the company of Bertraine, Noel had been dipping mighty deep at
some of those pall-mall hells. . . .

With a great deal of self-control, he laid the
matter aside. To betray his own anguish would
be to throw the matter into the hands of the gossips, not a fate relished for the Pellerins. He
turned his full attention back to Lady Jersey's inconsequential chatter.

Oblivious to the impending thunderclouds,
Miss Pellerin allowed herself to be led through
the steps of the cotillion by Mr. Woodville.
Looking up into his face, she allowed herself a
tiny smile and was rewarded with a reassuring

pressure against her hand. "You are the most beautiful female here tonight, you know," he said softly.

"Oh, no!" Elise immediately protested. "Charlotte is!"

To anyone else but the very prejudiced Mr. Woodville, this might have been true, but he merely shook his head. "And what's more, you are all the crack!"

To this, Elise was forced to sacrifice her dignity for laughter. "Oh, then at last I am quite fashionable!"

"Exactly so!" Mr. Woodville responded lazily. "And soon you shall create, no doubt, a fashion in which all the ladies will be seen to be concentrating with their utmost effort to rival your talent as an artist. Watercolors will be swept aside, and oils will become all the rage! Billy Turner had better make room for all the females who will be pressing to become artists."

Elise laughed and reluctantly allowed him to surrender her to Lord Brandamore, who was next upon the set.

By the second dance, a light country air, it was generally held that Lady Charlotte's ball for Miss Pellerin was an unqualified success, and that once again, the sparkling young widow was the paramount hostess of the ton.

Relinquishing Miss Pellerin to Sir Francis, Mr. Woodville tended to drift away from the festivities. Pausing for a word here and a greeting there, he scanned the ballroom most carefully, gradually making his way toward the card room, where he found the object of his pursuit.

The room was filled with card players, and it took several seconds for Mr. Woodville to pick out Noel Pellerin seated at a table with two of his other juniors, Mr. Chuffy Watham and young Viscount Deaver. They were playing three-handed deep basset at pound points, and Noel was dipping his cards almost wrecklessly, bidding against hands he knew he could not draw.

Mr. Woodville sauntered casually over to the table and greeted the company.

"Hullo! Will you make up our table, sir?" Noel demanded, his voice slightly edged with defiance.

Chuffy and Deaver both made room for him, and he sat down and cut the cards, dealing out swiftly. They played three or four hands without too much comment, although Woodville's eyes watched the pile of gold coins before Noel slowly drift in his own direction.

"Well, I'm in, sir!" young Watham exclaimed at last, tossing his cards upon the table. "I believe I'll go and seek feminine consolation in the ballroom." He pushed himself out from the table. "Frank?" he demanded of Lord Deaver.

"Oh, just when I was win—that is, yes! Very definitely seek out a dance! Miss Wilkes, m'fiancée, very notable girl!" he stammered, catching the glint in Woodville's eye.

Mr. Woodville smiled at Noel. It was not a particularly pleasant smile and it did not quite reach his eyes as his hands shuffled the pasteboards. "Pellerin? You seem to be in a gaming mood tonight. What say to you and me pursuing just a round or two of faro?"

Noel bit his lip, studying the cards spread on the table before him. As his hand reached for his empty glass, Woodville noticed that it was tremulous.

He signaled the waiter to bring another tray, and began to shuffle out the cards. "None of these chicken stakes, old friend!" he said grimly. "Let us, you and me, play for pound points! Perhaps your luck will change!"

From an inner pocket, Noel removed three coins, stacking them on the green felt table. He studied Mr. Woodville's pile, so much larger, and bit his lower lip. A feverish smile crossed his face. His eyes narrowed. "You don't like me much, do you?" he asked.

"On the contrary, I like you well enough!" Woodville replied, selecting a stack of three guineas and easing them out to the table. "Shall we play?" He handed the cards to Noel.

The boy seized them and began to shuffle, then dealt them each five cards, face down.

Mr. Woodville's hand caused him to smile. He watched as Noel slowly blanched and laid down his cards. "You—you win, sir!" he muttered, pushing his guineas across the table.

Mr. Woodville smiled again, scooping the guineas into a pile. "Shall we play again?" he asked.

Noel stared at the cards as if they had betrayed him. "You shall have to accept my vowels, sir! I—I have no more with me!"

Mr. Woodville's hands shuffled the cards. He regarded them seriously. "No. I do not think I will accept your vowels, Pellerin. I propose to make the stakes a little more interesting, if you please!"

Frightened brown eyes met his own.

Almost thoughtfully, Woodville dealt out the hand.

"W-what sort of stakes, sir?" Noel asked, barely suppressing the tremor in his voice.

"There was a list in my dispatch box, this morning, of certain key figures, shall we say, now located in the French government. I received word this afternoon that that list was missing." One card was slapped down upon the green felt. "In the hours between one and four, when I was engaged in a meeting with Lord Alvanley. Only one person was present in the office. And only one person had access to that box." He shot a look from beneath his brows at the boy, and another pasteboard slapped against the table.

Noel Pellerin laughed. The sound had a knife's edge, and he leaned back in his chair, his long fingers drumming on the table. "You are accusing *me*—no!" He flushed as crimson as his face had been pale before.

"I accuse no one," Mr. Woodville said smoothly. "I only state the facts." Slowly, he leaned forward, "Pellerin," he said in a different tone, "it's pretty well known that you've been playing for deep stakes of late . . ."

With a great deal of effort, Noel forced his lips to form a smile. "I—I had nothing to do with it. It's true that I've been on a cursed run of bad luck of late, but I shall come about!"

Woodville's brows rose slightly. "Again, I make no accusation. I am only stating the facts and drawing from them the conclusion that others will inevitably draw when this matter comes to light—as it must, and soon! The memorandum fortunately, is encoded, and it will take time for it to be placed into the hands of Boney's agents, and time more, still, to be in the hands of French Intelligence. But, if that slip of paper is placed in the proper hands, Pellerin, twelve men will die—and their deaths will make the guillotine look merciful indeed."

"I—I—this goes too far! You accuse me of stealing, sir! You have done nothing but harass me since I joined your office. Because I am French, you think that I am not to be trusted! This is outrageous! I know nothing of this memorandum! If you have not come down upon me about my personal habits, which are no business of yours, it has been about my—my associations!"

"If you're speaking of that harpy I pressed away from you at Covent Garden, think no more upon it! Mrs. Ridgely is well known for her ability to sink her talons into young men and bleed them dry."

Noel shook his head, impatient. "No—no! It's my friend Bertraine you do not like—as well as I! By God, sir, I ought to call you out!"

Since Mr. Woodville was a notable hand with both pistols and épée, and Noel was not, this threat was hollow indeed. But Woodville pressed forward. "If not for your sister and your uncle, and the respect I have for your family, you young whelp, I would take your bluff. In fact, Pellerin, I would like nothing better than to administer the whipping to you which your uncle should have administered when you were still in short coats! But you would do well to leave your uncle and sister out of this matter. Do you wish to drag them into what will surely be a very ugly scandal unless we can find some means to circumvent it?!"

"We?" Noel hissed, pressing advantage. "We! So, you admit that you might be at fault—that *your* carelessness might have possibly lost your precious memorandum!"

Mr. Woodville did not flinch. "I admit nothing. I only tell you what it would appear to be." A flicker of temper passed over him, and he clutched Noel's hand in his own, his fingers pressing into the boy's thin wrist. The awful smile lingered on his lips as he brought his face close to Noel's. "I think, dear boy, that you know more than you choose to tell me. And I think further that if that memorandum is not returned to the dispatch box, you will know what punishments His Majesty's government inflicts upon traitors!"

Noel broke loose from his grip and stood up. His dark, hollow eyes scanned Woodville's face "You hate me, don't you?" he whispered.

Mr. Woodville relaxed slightly. "On the contrary, dear boy, I like you well enough to want to save your neck from the gallows!" He spread his hands on the green baize table. "Noel, if you would make a clean breast of it, I could help you. Your debts are not such that they could not be straightened out, if you would but promise to cut closer in the future. I know that you have friends who do not feel that they owe their loyalty to England, but that they should—"

"I've heard enough!" Noel sputtered. Several players at nearby tables looked up from their games.

"For God's sake, keep your voice down. Would you have all the world know about this?" Mr. Woodville said quietly.

But Noel Pellerin had been pushed beyond his own strength. Roughly, he jammed his hands into his pockets, his eyes narrowed. "I don't admit to anything! Nothing! And you can't prove anything, either! D'you think I care so much for your dull jobs! I never wanted to go into government—it was my uncle and my sister who pushed you to hire me! By God, sir—you shall have my resignation in the morning!"

As he turned on his heel and stalked out of the room, Mr. Woodville's hand scooped up the cards, stacking the deck on the table. His face was thoughtful. After a few minutes, he too rose.

Instead of following Noel into the ballroom, Mr. Woodville sent word around to the stables for Jerry to have his phaeton ready as soon as possible.

The evening was three-quarters gone when Elise, breathless from an energetic waltz with Lord Torrance, begged him to fetch her a lemonade and retired to the side of the room, fanning herself as she watched Lady Charlotte and Lord Brandamore stand up for their second dance of the evening, cutting gracefully through the figures of the country dance.

Noel came up beside her so quietly that she almost jumped when his hand closed about her wrist. She was about to remonstrate with him when she saw that his face was set in an expression of extreme anguish. "Elise," he hissed, "I must have a word with you at once!"

Uncertainly, she allowed him to lead her away from the floor into one of the secluded alcoves, turning upon him as soon as they were out of the gaze of the curious. "Noel, what ever has happened to you? You look as if you'd seen a ghost! Are you quite well?" She peeled back her glove and laid her wrist against his forehead, but he brushed this gesture of concern away angrily, dabbing at his perspiring brow with his handkerchief. "Damn it, Elise, I am not sick! When will you stop coddling me as if I were in leading-strings!" he cried; then, seeing her expression, made some attempt to steel his countenance. "Hang it, Elise, how much money can you lay your hands on?" he demanded.

"M-money?" Elise repeated blankly.

Noel nodded fiercely. "I've tendered my resignation to Woodville! I shall leave immediately. Damme, if he thinks that he may accuse Prince d'Angelle of stealing his cursed memoranda, he will have to think again! Elise, he is odiously top-lofty and beyond bearing! Ever since I came to work at the Foreign Office, it has been one thing after another! He is always after me, Elise! It is past bearing! Well, Deaver and the rest may take his cavalier treatment, but I shan't! And all—all because I dug too deeply! Not but I won't come about all right, for there's a great goer I've been told about that's running at Newmarket, but I will not bear with being accused of stealing!"

With a sinking feeling, Miss Pellerin vainly attempted to sort out these utterances. Noel pushed his hands deeper into his pockets and glared at her as if she were at fault, continuing to mutter imprecations against Mr. Woodville that might have rendered him liable for slander if confined to a listener less discreet than his sister. When she attempted to be slightly enlightened, he only threw up his hands. "Females!" he exclaimed. "They understand nothing! Listen, Elise, I need money because I've got to rusticate for a while. At least until this thing blows over! If it weren't for—well, the man's a crack shot, or I'd call him out! Really I would! Woodville is accusing me of stealing a piece of paper from his damned dispatch box—and all because I was alone in the office from one 'til four! Actually, I wasn't because Emile dropped by, but Emile would no more steal a piece of paper than I would!"

Elise was beginning to unravel this tangled narrative. She clutched her fan tightly in her hand and stared at her brother, feeling as if all the precariously built happiness upon which she had sustained herself in the past month was suddenly being shaken out from beneath her feet by an earthquake of terrible proportions. "Mr. Woodville . . . accused you of stealing something?" she asked faintly.

"Damn, Elise, what have I been telling you? That's what he did! Some dashed list of spies or something! I won't have it, I tell you! Just because he don't like me, just because I'm French and the rest of 'em are the gentlemen's sons, I'm the one to blame! Any one of the lads could have swiped it, I tell you! But no, the blame must rest on me! Prince d'Angelle, a thief! Elise, it is beyond bearing!"

Elise looked at the tips of her satin slippers, miserable thoughts crowding her mind. How could she have cherished *feelings* for a man so obviously prejudiced against her own kind of people! It was beyond bearing! Simply because one was French and a refugee, and poor, one was suspect! Noel was irresponsible at times, she would admit, but dishonest, never! He had been too finely bred in a sense of his honor to ever steal, no matter how desperate the situation. "WHY would he think you would steal his terrible memorandum?" Elise demanded.

"My debts, of course!" Noel replied. "Don't you see, Elise—"

"*Ah, beauty fair, thy light outshines all these stars so hea'nly placed—*"

Noel and Elise both whirled about toward the entrance, where Emile Bertraine, a faint smile playing about his lips, stood watching them.

Elise sighed with relief. "Emile! You are just the person we need! Thank God, you have come! Noel is in the devil's own tangle!"

Emile sauntered into the alcove. His eyes flickered appreciatively over Elise's form and dress. "How much more beautiful you have become since Lady Charlotte took you under her wing, Elise, *ma petite!* I believe I shall have to offer for you one of these days. Will you dance with me, or are you quite filled up with all your English suitors?"

Elise tossed her head. "Oh, Emile, do be serious! This is important. Noel is in serious trouble!"

"All because of that top-lofty stepson of Lady Charlotte's, I am to believe?" Emile questioned lightly. "Come, Noel, tell all, and let us see what we may do!"

Briefly and tersely, Noel explained the situation that had been enacted in the card room. With all the faith in the world, Elise watched her old friend's face. He looked very grave indeed.

"And so, he's threatening to *hang* me if the dashed memorandum is not returned! And you know, Emile, you know that I didn't steal it, and what's more I don't have the faintest idea where it is! You were there. You know that I was working on some translations all afternoon——"

Emile made a small sound in the back of his throat, shaking his head. "The situation looks very grave, does it not?" he asked. "No, Noel, I know that you could not have taken Woodville's accursed paper. For all we know, he may have misplaced it, or even extricated it himself, or knows who really took it, and is seeking to cover up for one of his friends by accusing you——"

"Exactly," Elise said dully. "Because Noel is French, he might as well be fair game!"

"Exactly so!" Emile replied sadly. "Too often,

too often have I seen *nos émigrés* unjustly accused of selling information to Napoleon's spies. And in that work, Noel, perhaps it would be better if no one knew that I was there that afternoon! It would only seem to be collaboration that you stole the memorandum!"

Noel nodded glumly. "True. But what, Emile, am I to do?"

"We must tell Uncle at once!" Elise exclaimed. "He will know what we must do!"

Emile laid a hand on her arm, shaking his head. "No, Elise, you must not involve your uncle in this! It would surely affect his health!" He drew his brows down thoughtfully, regarding the Pellerins. "This is a havey-cavey business and no mistake! Think, Noel. Have you ever seen this memorandum? Is there any way whatsoever that Woodville could connect you with it?"

Noel scrawled and shook his head, barely concealing the fact that he was a frightened young boy. "No! Until he accused me, I'd never even known that it existed! Damme, I'm not a thief!"

"Of course you are not, and it was extremely odious of Mr. Woodville to say that you were! How could he be so—so—" Elise twisted her fan between her fingers, feeling a cold sense of betrayal and pain.

"I have heard rumors," Emile murmured unhappily. "The usual sort of things one hears, when one's, er, acquaintances are as varied as mine own . . ."

Both Pellerins looked at him. He shifted uncomfortably. "Well, in my profession, you know, one slips back and forth, and one . . . knows a great many people. Politics have never interested me, you know that. I'm that rare thing," he laughed, "an honest rogue; but there are others, you know, not quite so honest. I have heard rumors that Mr. Woodville had been making certain inquiries on the other side of the Channel. Apparently, Sir Vincent left him dashed little—most of his estate went to Lady Charlotte, y'know! *C'est dommage,* but there you have it!"

Elise's pain was beginning to twist into a sort of white fury in her heart. "That—that, oh, how reprehensible!" she hissed. "And of course, he would accuse Noel!" And offer me a carte blanche in time, no doubt, she thought, and her anger burned hotter still.

"This is all very right and fine!" Noel sputtered. "But what am I to do? My neck stands in the gallows!"

Emile frowned. "You must give me time, *mes amis!* Perhaps, just perhaps, I may know how and where to go to trace this memorandum! As you know, I have many many friends who are not the sort of people I would wish you to deal with—but if I can, I shall seek to obtain this piece of paper before it can cross the Channel.

"You see, a certain very important person for whom I once rendered a service—a very small matter, I assure, of a word in his ear about a so-called friend who was cheating at cards at Watier's—has asked me if I would develop my friendships in certain, er, segments of the town; apparently, there has been some suspicion in Woodville's direction for quite some time. . . . But you must say nothing, do you understand? News of this would endanger my life, and the safety of others. Trust me!" He smiled reassuringly.

"I—I had no idea that you—" Noel stammered.

Emile smiled and shrugged. "I am not quite so disreputable as I seem, *hein, mon petit?* But no mind! You must trust me! I shall make all right!"

"Dear Emile! I knew that you could not possibly be as—as black as you have been painted by the world!" Elise caught her friend's hand up in her own. "How—how very good a friend you have been to us! As always, we depend upon you!"

Emile allowed his own hand to close about hers. He clasped Noel's shoulder. "*Pour le prince et la princesse, c'est tout!*" he said warmly. "I shall undertake at once to make certain inquiries. A word here, a scrap of information there, and I think we may have our Woodville trapped!"

"But what must we do in the meantime! By

God, I'd like to plant that rogue a facer!" Noel cried.

"Nothing," Emile said quietly. "You must do nothing at all. You must, Noel, continue on at the Foreign Office as if nothing is amiss. And you, Elise must stay on here, although I know that very feeling must repulse at living in such proximity to a man who would send your brother to the gallows!"

Noel mumbled in protest, but Elise squared her shoulders, holding her head high. "We will do as you say, Emile, will we not, *mon frère?*" She demanded, taking Noel's hand and holding it tightly.

Noel nodded. The tension had not left his countenance, but his eyes seemed to his sister to convey some sense of relief and trust as he gazed upon the older man. "We must trust Emile," he mumbled. "Emile always knows best!"

M. Bertraine's eyes flickered over them both. A slight smile played across his face, and he jerked his sleek head slightly. "I shall do all that is in my power," he promised gravely. "But" —and his eyes seemed to be penetrating their souls— "you must trust me completely."

"We do!" Noel exclaimed.

"Of course, Emile. How could you doubt us?" Elise asked. "Dear Emile! Who else could we depend upon to rescue us from yet another scrape?"

Emile nodded, satisfied. "Now, you must not

worry, *mes chers amis*. Emile will set all to rights within forty-eight hours. That, at least, I will promise you!" His face turned serious. "Now, can you go on as if nothing is amiss?"

The Pellerins agreed. M. Bertraine tucked Elise's arm into his own. "*Eh bien!* Elise, you will come and dance with me?"

She smiled up into his face. "My dear old friend," she replied in French, her eyes narrowing, "nothing would give me more pleasure!" The defiant ring in her voice almost suppressed the agitation beneath her tones.

Chapter Eight

For Elise, the day after the ball was one of stunned and reluctant misery. Nothing, she reflected unhappily, could have destroyed her new-found pleasure in life more than the contemplation of the falseness of the gentleman who had, within the space of twenty-four hours, turned from a hero into the vilest sort of villain. Never had she been more miserable or more cast down than those sullen morning hours in which she lay abed after a restless and fitful space of would-be slumber, contemplating the gray rain which splattered upon the panes of her bedroom window.

Such was her agony that she felt herself unable to face Lady Charlotte for several hours

succeeding the lady's awakening after the rigors
of entertaining three hundred persons until the
dawn hours. How could she possibly confront
her dear friend without some measure of the betrayal slipping through her best-erected defenses?
Elise wondered. And what would her dear friend
think when she discovered that her beloved Sir
Vincent's son was a traitor? The thought did not
easily bear contemplation, and when Miss Pellerin pleaded a headache as her excuse for refusing to accompany Lady Charlotte and Lord
Brandamore upon an expedition to Bond Street,
it was not entirely a falsehood.

Every sentiment within Elise's person was in
revolt, and yet how could she mistrust the facts
as laid before her by Emile Bertraine? Noel was
in trouble, and the force of long habit, as well as
an implicit trust in her oldest friend, would not
permit her to entertain any thought other than
that set forth in Emile's suppositions. Twist and
turn logic and reason in her head as she might,
she could find nothing that would excuse Mr.
Woodville's conduct. The idea that Noel could
possibly be wrong was outside her ken; he was as
incapable as she herself of committing so grave a
crime. That Emile might have sought to twist the
truth to suit his own ends was impossible; she
had known him all of her life, and indeed, without hesitation would have trusted him with the
precious burden of it unquestionably. There was
no way out of the tangle, she thought miserably.

Woodville, the man in whom she had reposed the fondest of hopes, who had outwardly shown her every courtesy and kindness, was capable of the blackest sort of hypocrisy. Even as he was entertaining her in the most genteel fashion, his mind must have been given over to schemes for the downfall of her brother. And what better dupe would an experienced man find than a young and impetuous boy, barely down from college, anxious to crack his experience upon the town in the most time-honored ways of all young men? It was beyond mere pain; it was a betrayal of the vilest sort, for Woodville had found a vulnerable place within her heart, a place she had never known existed until he had discovered it within her secret self. . . .

The afternoon lengthened into evening, and not even Miss Elder's extremely condescending offer to bathe her temples in hartshorn and lavender water would rouse Elise from her anxious lethargy. Huddled upon her bed, with an unread novel cast off at her side, she anxiously awaited some message that would mean success or failure, and yet nothing but silence maintained itself in the house.

Toward the early evening, she heard the unmistakable sounds of a carriage before the house, but it was only Lady Charlotte returned from her shopping expedition in time to change her clothes for a dinner party.

Calling through the door, Charlotte kindly inquired if her friend meant to rouse herself for the evening's party. "For you know, dear, that Sir Francis will be most disappointed not to see you in the company," she whispered.

"I—I can't," Elise replied in a muffled voice. "Please, Charlotte, do not ask me to do so!"

Lady Charlotte inclined her head to one side, staring at the panels of the door with rather more thoughtfulness than was her norm. "I think something is troubling Elise," she said cautiously.

Elder shook her head. "I think Miss had too much champagne last night. And you know how that may effect a lady not used to excessive spirits, ma'am!"

Lady Charlotte, satisfied with this explanation, charged Elise to stay upon her bed and try to sleep, and promised that she would monitor her friend upon her return late that evening. Receiving some noncommittal remark in return, she seemed satisfied, and immediately turned her head toward the choice between teal blue and lilac silk for the evening's course of events.

If Elise had somewhere inside herself cherished the fantasy that she would be able to confront Mr. Woodville upon his return home that evening, she was disappointed. The master, Elder informed her as she removed an untouched tray, had left directly after the ball last night and was not expected home for several days. Since Mr. Woodville's valet had loftily confirmed the household's suspicions that his master was engaged upon work too delicate for the understanding of the servant's hall, Elder was also swift to dispense this information to Elise, perhaps because the dresser privately considered that Miss had set her sights too high when she aimed for such a gentleman as Mr. Woodville.

Elise accepted this information with more relief than meekness, although Elder was able to carry the tray belowstairs and loftily inform the rest that Miss was about due for a good dosing of "reality in the polite world." Basile, who had formed a liking for Miss Pellerin, informed milady's dresser in repressive accents that them as laughed loudest laughed last, a sentiment privately endorsed by Coe and two maids, who would, of course, never dream of intruding their views into the conversation of two of the more important persons in the hall.

But this altercation, as icy as it may have been, was sufficient to occupy both Elder and Basile in matters that would not take them abovestairs, where a chance encounter might have led to a more serious exchange. With Miss laid out upon her bed, the master and milady both gone out, there seemed to be no cause for any of the servants to venture abovestairs, and so, they were denied the interesting sight of Miss Pellerin, haggard-faced and clothed only in her dressing gown and slippers, making her way into the library where her painting kit was still spread out by the window.

With trembling fingers, she lifted the linen from the half-completed painting she had laid aside the day before the ball. By candlelight, she would see that the features of the portrait were somewhat softened. Ordinarily, this might have pleased her, for the work, having been executed without the knowledge or posing of the sitter, had been executed from memory and careful observation, and in a rather hopeful, almost daydreaming manner that must have been, she reflected, positively girlishly foolish.

She held the candelabra higher and stepped back, her eyes narrowed, to observe the very credible portrait of Mr. Woodville which had been the source of so much pleasure before. But the anxiety which had driven her to the library to view it just one more time, and the ethic which had pronounced that working out one's nerves upon canvas rather than in the idleness of waiting upon the pleasure of men to come home from their roistering prevailed; and without much thought of what she intended to do, she began to work her pigments with linseed oil, intent upon having her own small vengeance upon the man who had betrayed her so terribly.

Gaunt-faced and hollowed-eyed, she employed her brushes with a fury for several hours. And when at last her nerves gave way to utter exhaustion, she stepped back to view the changes.

Before, Mr. Woodville's countenance had been smiling most pleasantly upon the viewer, his handsome eyes betraying that rare smile, his mouth set in a way that might have betrayed the laughter rising to his lips. But now, he had taken a diabolic cast; the eyes were sinister, the lips tight and secretive, as if he viewed the world with doubt and suspicions. It was but the work of a few minutes to change a coat of somber buff to a flame red stain cape, and only a few brush strokes to add horns to the black curls. From angel to devil was a matter of transition, and it gave her no small sense of grim satisfaction that she had been able to convey upon her canvas the feeling she bore toward the sitter. From *Mr. Woodville* to *Mephistopheles* was a transition of her talents. *A likeness taken by Miss Pellerin, from life*, she added to herself and could not repress the rather terrible smile which rose to her own lips. Thus would she avenge, she thought. If her uncle had been present, he would have known that particular look all too well and would doubtless have protested vehemently. But Comte Auguste was safe in his own bed, halfway across town, and Miss Pellerin was allowed to gloat as she pleased for several minutes before snuffing out the candles and carrying the small canvas up the stairs to her own bedchamber, where she faced it before the fire in the grate.

It had been her experience that a light coat of paint would generally dry out in the outer layers

enough to travel if exposed to heat overnight.
And in the morning, she had her own plans for
that piece of work. It would be the instrument of
her revenge.

With the light from the coal flames throwing
an eerie, almost hellish, glow upon the painting,
its exhausted executioner fell into a deep sleep,
troubled by unhappy dreams.

It was just past ten, and Lady Charlotte was
still abed, when Miss Pellerin, her walking dress
of apricot muslin worn beneath a spencer of
bronze sarcenet ornamented with epaulets and
frogs, a very fetching Russian cap set upon her
dark curls and sturdy walking boots of orange
jean upon her feet, descended the stairs with a
canvas package under her arm. Despite this fashionable toilette, the not totally uninterested eye
of Coe was able to discern that Miss was not in
her best fettle, and when she demurred his escort
upon her walk, it was only the most benevolent
and fatherly protestations of Basile that no lady
would walk abroad in London unattended that
pursuaded her to accept Coe's presence a respectful three paces behind her.

Miss Pellerin was by no means pleased to have
the footman trailing in her wake, particularly
since she labored under the strong suspicion that
her movements would instantly be communicated
to Mr. Woodville; but as she made her progress
through the streets between Upper Mount and

Bond, she was glad for the tall, silent shadow behind her. More than once, a carter or a workman cast a roguish glance in her direction, and she had the strong feeling that if not for the footman, she might have been the recipient of some most unwelcome advances.

However, she was able to reach the discreet brownstone townhouse which sheltered Comte Pellerin's galleries without mishap, and instructed Coe to await her return in the hallway.

No one could have accused Miss Pellerin of an uneasy temper. In general, she was possessed of a sanguine disposition, and a shrewd sense of logic and proportion. But a heart, which has long lain dormant and is suddenly, and somewhat against its possessor's will, activated by sentiments which recognize none of the elements of reason, is prone to force acts of passionate sensibility upon even the most sensible of human beings. And Miss Pellerin was no exception to this rule, for the anger which had impelled her to alter the portrait of Mr. Woodville moved upon tides of such force that she continued this last, grand gesture through to its conclusion.

Unfortunately, Comte Auguste was a guest at Fonthill Abbey, or his reason might have prevailed over his niece's impetuosity; but as a guest of the eccentric collector Mr. Beckford, he was safely removed from the premises.

Miss Pellerin walked through the long gallery, past the current exhibition of the works of Mr.

Farington, and straight on into the smaller gallery in the rear, where the melancholy Jean-Claude was supervising the hanging of her own pictures. Seeing the artist, the saturnine Frenchman immediately grew both defensive and obsequious from long practice with dealings with persons of volatile and creative dispositions.

"*Alors,* ma'mselle, as you can see, we hang your paintings; I follow M. le Comte's instructions to the letter, the landscapes of Oxfordshire just so, the still lifes here—" He began hurrying toward Miss Pellerin in an attempt to block her view of the hanging in anticipation of a display of artistic temperament which he was long since used to receiving from painters who objected to the methods of displaying their works.

With a cursory glance at the workmen, Elise nodded, turning her most devastating smile upon her uncle's assistant. "Of course, Jean-Claude," she said in rapid French, "and everything is most excellent. You are always to be depended upon to know how works may be shown to advantage!"

Without giving him time to recover from this unexpected attitude, she continued on in an amazing, if conscious, imitation of Lady Charlotte at her most persuasive. "There is only one thing—so silly of me not to have this ready when the show will open tomorrow evening—but you must help me! And I know you will, Jean-Claude, because you are always to be depended upon!" This was followed by what Noel Pellerin would have characterized as his sister's most roguish look, always certain to bring recalcitrant tradesmen, surly porters and other reluctant individuals around to her way of thinking that the meat must be of a better cut, that taking one from Little Clarendon to the High was not impossible in such a very little rainstorm, and, of course, one would be glad to make room in the inn for such a lovely and gracious lady, even if it meant moving two gentlemen into a chamber hired for one. Jean-Claude might be a misogynist, but even that was of no avail against Miss Pellerin's charm, for he was already leaning forward in in anticipation of her bidding as she held out the canvas-wrapped package toward him. "So silly of me not to have it completed with the rest . . . but such an integral part of the show, you see . . . You will be able to frame it and hang it somewhere, I trust?" she was murmuring, and before Jean-Claude had as much as a chance to protest that it would quite destroy the balance of landscape and still life, he was already agreeing to immediately make up a frame and mount the work himself, without so much as opening the wrappings.

When he bowed her out upon the waiting Coe, he was all smiles and best wishes for her opening, assuring her that she possessed a rare talent, and that her work would surely win her a rare female nomination to the Academy.

With the sort of cool confidence that only the most white hot of angers can produce, Miss Pellerin graciously thanked him for his compliments, assured him that she reposed every confidence in his ability to mount her show, and took her leave, a small, tight and very malicious smile transfixing her face. Whatever else was to occur, she was certain now that she would have her revenge.

It was cold comfort, indeed, but any sort of action, she thought bitterly, was better than waiting helplessly for some resolution to the unhappy situation in which she found herself. She hoped that by the time of her opening exhibition, Emile would have put all to rights, and she would enjoy her quiet triumph when Noel's wrongs were redressed and Mr. Woodville had seen that she had exposed him to the world for what he really was. Cold comfort, she thought unhappily, not daring to examine her motives too closely.

She threw up her chin against the drizzly spring morning, almost defiantly. The wind might whip too closely through her fashionable muslin dress, but it could never be as cold as the arctic chill in her heart.

"Ah, there you are!" Lady Charlotte called from the morning room when Elise came into the hallway. "Wherever have you been, Elise?" she asked. "We have a regiment of morning callers, and half of them, I think, will die of a broken heart if they do not see y— Elise, my love, do you feel quite well?" Concerned with her friend's haggard appearance, Lady Charlotte laid a cool hand against Elise's fevered cheeks.

Elise gazed upon her friend's pretty, vacuous face in some distress, not untouched by her expressions of concern. For a moment, it was upon her lips to blurt out the entire, terrible story and repose upon her friend's confidence, but at that moment, Lord Brandamore strolled into the doorway and raised his quizzing glass.

"I say, Miss Pellerin," he drawled. "You don't look all the thing! In fact, you look dashed temperish to me! Was it the oysters we ate night before last at the ball? I think they made me a trifle queasy! Dashed bad thing for a female to be going about not looking her best. You ought to lie down!"

"Of course!" Lady Charlotte agreed. "You ought to be upon your bed, Elise, and not prancing upon the town! Dear me, I have teased you all out of bloom with this raking about the town, and now I have only myself to blame if you come down with some horrid influenza or other!"

Elise shook her head, trying to force a smile to rise to her face. "I only stepped about to the gallery to see how my exhibition was being mounted. The show will open tomorrow night, you know, and I wanted to be certain—"

"Of course!" Lord Brandamore said. "That rips it! Charl', send Miss Pellerin off to bed at

once, and send round for Dr. Monro— She must
be fit for the opening!"

"Then you must not ease yourself with even
thinking of coming out with me this afternoon to
Lady Lawrence's," Charlotte continued, undoing
the strings of Elise's hat in a most maternal fashion. "But take yourself off to bed at once!"

It was only with the most strident protests that
she was only in need of some rest, and not at all
of the services of the most fashionable doctor in
London, that Elise was able to avoid a visit from
that medical man.

In a very short time, she was settled upon her
couch with a number of shawls and comforters
wrapped about her, resisting solicitous offers to
have her temples bathed with lavender water,
and burnt feathers waved beneath her nose. No,
she would not take a few drops of laudanum in a
glass of hot wine, and she did not care for a hot
brick against her feet, and please, would they all
just let her be for a while?

So great was Elise's guilt that she could not
feel comfortable in what she could only see as
the grossest deception of Lady Charlotte, and she
was glad when that kind person at last left her to
her own devices, but only, it must be added, with
the greatest reluctance, to visit Lady Lawrence.

Elise lay restlessly upon her bed, staring up at
the ceiling, listening to the hours ticking away on
the mantel clock. It seemed as if she would never
hear the words she longed for.

Surely Emile must have failed, and even at that moment, Noel must be reposing in Newgate. Never had she felt so helpless; accustomed to doing for herself, it was hard indeed for her to believe that every avenue of action was closed off to her and that she would only wait in helpless prostration.

Several times, she rose from her uneasy repose to attempt to compose herself, pacing restlessly back and forth in her chamber, fighting away the images of Mr. Woodville that rose in her mind. It was beyond bearing!

And each time, she would return to her bed to sob with helpless tears of rage and frustration, alternating between deep despondency and feverish elation. Not even the pleasure that she had so long dreamed of, having her own exhibition of painting, could quite save her from the anguish she felt that dreary London afternoon.

Several times, Elder knocked upon the door and offered her assistance, and each time she received the muffled reply that Miss did not care for a bowl of gruel, or a little weak tea and toast.

It was just past four, when Elise was certain that she would go mad, that Elder rapped again upon her door, announcing a message had been borne over from a M. Bertraine, and that it was of the utmost urgency that she reply.

Elise flew from the bed to the door, seizing the folded and sealed letter as if it were her last hope

of salvation. With trembling fingers she ripped
up the seal and scanned the paper.

> My dear Elise—
> I have in hand that which you
> desire. Can you meet me at the Red
> Lion at six o'clock? Bring a valise; we
> shall be out of London by nightfall. N.
> shall accompany you, so do not fear
> for your propriety.
>
> Ever,
>
> E. Bertraine

Elise folded the document with trembling fingers, doing all that she could to suppress the relief and excitement which flooded through her.
"Please tell the messenger that the answer is
yes," she told Elder, keeping her voice as steady
as she possibly could.

But still, the dresser eyed her sharply, and it
took a great deal of effort for her to keep her
thoughts from appearing upon her own countenance. When Elise turned with a questioning
eye to see her still standing in the doorway, she
bowed a reluctant curtsy and strode down the
hallway.

At the head of the stairs, however, she paused,
her trained dresser's ears catching the unmistakable sounds of a heavy portmanteau's brass
latches, and the rustle of dresses being removed

from a wardrobe. Nodding to herself with grim satisfaction, she relayed the message to Coe, and proceeded belowstairs to inform Basile that she, for one, had no idea what the world was coming to, but there was something havey-cavey afoot, or she would be called a Green Jane.

Basile solicited enlightenment upon this point, and as Miss Elder proceeded to gratify his curiosity, Jerry, sitting in the chimney corner making short work of a sweetmeat he had filched from the pastry table when Alphonse's back was turned, also pricked up his ears.

He was a small lad for his age and used to moving stealthily. It was but the work of a few minutes for him to ease himself out of the doorway to the mews and start to run, as fast as his legs could carry him, toward King's Commons.

As she blindly stuffed items into her portmanteau, Miss Pellerin's disorganized faculties permitted her to exercise neither her common sense nor consideration of what she might ordinarily have found to be a most unusual request, even from such an adventurer as Emile Bertraine. Years of rescuing Noel from the consequences of his follies had inured her to the most inconvenient situations, and she was only thankful that the most sordid aspects of his current tangle had been removed from her hands by the wordly M. Bertraine. If, from time to time, hot tears spilled upon her feverish hands, she was able to dismiss this unwanted display of emotion as the release of pent-up anxiety, rather than any sense of disappointment from the unexpected role played in this situation by a certain gentleman.

The clock was moving toward half past the hour when, wrapped in her merino cloak trimmed with beaver, and clutching her portmanteau in one hand, Elise cautiously drew the bolt on her door and glanced up and down the empty hallway. Behind her, she had left a brief and tear-stained note for Lady Charlotte, saying only that she had been called away by "a dire emergency" concerning Noel, and "no matter what happened," she was still Charlotte's "loving friend" Elise, who would always be grateful for the "pleasures her dearest Charlotte had shared with such an ungrateful wretch."

The servants, fortunately, were all at their dinner in the hall, and she was able to move delicately down the stairs and out the door without her orange jean boots making as much as a sound.

When the door closed behind her she breathed a sigh of relief, drawing the hood of her cardinal up about her head and moving through the gray drizzle toward the hack stand on the corner.

She chose the first jarvey in the line, an ancient and decrepit vehicle, drawn by a spavined nag and manned by a surly-looking individual with a scarlet proboscis. She gave her directions in such a melancholy tone that the hack was forced to inquire several times as to the precise nature of her address.

As the carriage rumbled away into the fog, the hack muttering beneath his breath about Tragedy Jills, a small, sharp-faced figure in a linsey coat moved out from his vantage point behind the railings of a nearby mansion, watching the hack lumbering into the fog. He mumbled the direction the hackney had repeated, then dashed across the wet cobblestones to the opposite side of the street, where a black barouche sat waiting. Scrambling up into the box beside the driver, an individual garbed in a coat of no less than sixteen capes, his lower face muffled by a scarf and a flat-crowned beaver drawn down over his eyes, the small person repeated the direction once again, and seemed gratified when his companion reached inside his coat and touched the butt of a lethal-looking pistol, as if to assure himself that it was indeed there.

The Red Lion was not an inn much patronized by persons of quality. During the brief Peace of '02, it had served as a posting house on the Dover-London Road; but not even the faintest trace of this glory seemed to remain with it, for it was a dank and ill-lit place, smelling strongly of old tobacco smoke and stale gin. Such trade as it now served, it seemed to Elise as she reluctantly left the minimal safety of the hack and stepped into the mud of the yard, seemed to be either persons of determinedly bucolic aspect, or such individuals of very low station in life as she had never encountered within the circles in which she traveled. She did not meet the curious, almost greedy stares of the loungers in the yard and she was grateful that she had worn her old cardinal, for she was of the strong suspicion that any toilette more grand would have seriously jeopardized her passage into the inn's doorway. As it was, a small boy in a ragged nankeen shirt, his nose apparently afflicted with a perpetual drip, blocked her way with an outstretched hand, and a scruffy-looking dog sniffed suspiciously at her hems. Almost automatically, she pressed a coin into the urchin's hand, and the child darted away without a word of thanks, closely pursued by several other ragged children, obviously out to best him for this treasure. This incident, rather than rousing any of the slothful loungers at the door, seemed to afford them the greatest amusement, and it was fortunate for Miss Pellerin that she did not comprehend their strong city dialects as they commented upon her aspect.

A slatternly female in a very dirty apron and mobcap was leaning against the bar in the taproom, idly pushing a filthy rag back and forth across the stained counter as she flirted with an unshaven individual in greenish-looking bombazine coat. Both turned to stare at Elise as she

closed the door behind her, their eyes flickering
with only the briefest of surprises as they appraised her appearance.

Elise took a deep breath. The smell of stale air
was even stronger within closed rooms, and she
felt a strong urge to turn and run. "If you
please," she began, "where may I find M. Bertraine?"

The barmaid drew a flaccid arm across her
nose, staring at Elise long after any interest
would have seemed necessary. Slowly, she flung
out her arm in the general direction of the dark
passageway toward the rear of the house. "Iffen
you means that Frog—'e's in the back parlor!
An' the master says there's to be no hanky-panky
'ere, mind! This is a respectable place!" she
added in a snickering voice. The man in the
bombazine coat chuckled unpleasantly, and Elise
had the oddest sensation that he was mentally examining her figure through her clothes.

Without a word, her cheeks flaming, she
gathered up her skirts in one hand and retreated
down the corridor. Since there was only one
door, she raised her hand and rapped upon the
scratched panels sharply with her knuckles, holding her breath against the musty stench.

After what seemed like an eternity to her, the
doorway opened into an ill-lit room, and Emile's
long, dark face floated before her.

"Ah, *ma petite*," he said softly. "Come in,

come in. I am glad that you came. You must forgive this place, but it was the best that I could do."

"Emile!" She breathed with relief. "Thank God! What sort of a place is this? Do you have the memorandum? Where is Noel?"

As her eyes adjusted to the darkness, she could make out the single table and two chairs in the room, and the tallow candle burning low in its socket. Behind her, Emile shut and locked the door, dropping the key into his pocket.

Elise was far too distracted to notice these procedures. As he advanced upon her, she frowned. "Emile, please, I shall go mad if you do not tell me! Do you have the memorandum? And why did I have to bring a portmanteau? And where is Noel?"

Bertraine smiled lazily. "Dear, impetuous Elise, such a loving sister. I only hope that you will make as loving a wife!"

Elise frowned. "Emile, I don't understand. Where is the—"

"—memorandum, your dear brother, and why are you packed for an overnight journey?" He laughed, holding up his hands. For the first time, in the candlelight, she noted how well-manicured the nails were. "I shall attempt to answer each of your questions singly, *ma petite,* and that way, there will be no more of this. The memorandum is in my pocket." He patted his breast significantly, and Elise did not quite like his smile.

Some uneasy feeling began to push its way into her consciousness. "Exactly where it has been all the while since I abstracted it from the dispatch box in Woodville's office. I had only to wait until Noel's back was turned, you see, to make my move. The poor boy let slip a great deal of information in his cups. One only had to feign, you understand, the slightest interest in all his many wrongs for him to spill out his heart to his dear friend Emile." Bertraine laughed unpleasantly, and Elise drew back a step, regarding him with a puzzled frown.

"To answer your next question: Noel, I imagine, is, even at this moment, being taken from Woodville's office by the magistrates for questioning about the abstraction of this document—"

"No!" Elise heard her voice somewhere very far away.

Bertraine shrugged. "*Mais oui, ma petite.* After all, everyone thinks that he stole it to sell to Napoleon's agents to pay his unfortunate gaming debts."

"Emile—" Shock, grief and betrayal rose up in Elise's breast. Suddenly, she started toward the doorway, frantically twisting the unyielding knob.

"Locked," Bertraine said simply. "Perhaps it would be better if you calmed down and listened to me, Elise, since it was for you that I did all this."

"Me?" Elise demanded. "Emile, how could you—? Noel, my brother—"

"Has been nothing but a burden to all of us since he was out of short coats. You will be better off without him," Bertraine shrugged. "After all, when we are married, I will not want to be continually rescuing Noel from his silly scrapes. . . ."

Elise hammered at the doorway, kicking the panels, but they were solidly fitted.

Behind her Emile chuckled softly. "No good, *ma petite*. The landlord has been well bribed. He thinks that you and I are, shall we say, a couple of lovers, and that you are a trifle reluctant to surrender to my advances. Amazing how solidly these old buildings are put together. Not much sound escapes. Now, to answer your third question, *ma petite,* you have brought your overnight things because you and I are going to France— where Napoleon is more than willing to restore to you all your lands and titles. Again, you will be the Princesse d'Angelle. And when Noel is hanging at Tyburn for treason, you will fall heir to all of the old d'Angelle estates; but I, of course, as your husband, will control the purse strings. And I am certain that the emperor will smile upon our marriage, for all the services I have rendered the empire will make me a hero of no mean repute."

"I'll never marry you!" Elise hissed. "Never!

How could you dare to expect that I would marry my brother's murderer, a traitor—?"

"Traitor? Patriot, I think they shall call me in France. This memorandum will finish off my career as a double agent. I would have waited to propose to you in the accepted, romantic fashion, but that foolish *anglaise* woman insisted upon bringing you out into society, casting you in the way of such rivals as Sir Francis and Lord Torrance and . . . Woodville. I knew that I must make my move rather more impetuously than I wished to do—curse that female, for I knew if nothing else were cast into your way, you would have accepted my suit easily. But Woodville, I knew he would be a prize hard to resist—and his attentions toward you were entirely too close. So, you see, I had to do it."

"But you are our friend! You have always been our friend, Emile! How could you?"

He shrugged, and his eyes narrowed dangerously. "Perhaps because I do not like these English, perhaps because I am tired of poverty. I have the tastes of an *aristo*, and none of the money to support them on. When I am your husband, when you are restored to your rights and glory in France, *ma petite*, you will thank me. And by your compliance, you may yet save your brother from the hangman's noose." He spoke casually, and yet Elise sensed the steel beneath his words.

Slowly, she sank into a chair. "How?" she asked.

"Come with me willingly, and I shall leave behind a second document" —again he touched his breast pocket—"explaining just how I abstracted the dreadful little piece of paper. That will save Noel's life. But I shall only leave it behind if you will come with me. Think, Elise. Think of the glory that waits you. To be *la princesse d'Angelle* again, under the glorious reign of the emperor! Your family titles, your lands, your wealth—all restored to you! The rights to which you were born—all yours!"

Elise closed her eyes. From somewhere deep in her memory, she saw again that hot July day, the ancient Paris streets, the platform erected in the square, the sickening smell of blood hanging in the still air, the glittering blade rising still wet with blood—the sickening sound it made as it fell against—

"No," she whispered, shaking her head. "No. Never back to France, never."

"Would you rather Noel died?"

"I trusted you once, and you betrayed me, Emile," she sighed. "How am I to trust you again?"

"You only have my word. Come. It was fated that we should marry one day. Look at all the things I offer you. And Noel will live. But only if you come to France with me, a willing bride.

You may place the document into the receiving office with your own hands. It is already addressed to your Mr. Woodville."

Elise's head snapped forward as if she had been slapped. She was trapped. There was nothing else she could do. Noel must be saved.

"Very well," she said hoarsely, beyond tears or hope.

Emile nodded. Reverently, he picked up her hands and kissed them. "You will be happy, I promise you. In time, when you walk through the glorious court of Bonaparte, you will come to understand and appreciate what I have done for you. No more of this life as a poor churchmouse. Before you there lie riches and honor and glory—"

"Very well, I said I should go!" Elise exclaimed. "Only let us be quick about it. Give me the document, and I shall make haste to post it off."

"On our way," Bertraine smiled, pulling her to her feet. "Come, I have a chaise waiting for us. Our boat will sail from Dover on the dawn tide!"

Satisfied that his prisoner would cooperate, he opened the door and led her down the corridor. Elise moved as if in a dream, knowing not if she slept.

What happened next seemed almost as if it were a dream, for it all seemed to go so very slowly, almost as if it were some grotesque ballet.

He was standing in the doorway, she knew it was *he*, for who else in all of London was possessed of a buff driving-coat of sixteen capes? Somewhere, she heard the barmaid screaming, she saw the pistol he removed from beneath his coat. She saw his mouth moving, heard his words, though they seemed to come from a great distance away. And she knew, then, that Christian Woodville would somehow save her.

Beside her, Bertraine froze, but only for a second. Even as she was calling out his name, Bertraine was grasping her rudely, thrusting her in front of him. She felt the cold steel of Emile's pistol against her cheek, the cruel grasp of his fingers digging into her waist.

"Christian!" she cried.

The pressure of the cold steel barrel against her cheek increased. She could feel his hand trembling, and knew with a terrible certainty that he meant to kill her—Emile, who had always been her friend, meant to kill her. . . .

Woodville was talking to him, advancing step by step down the narrow corridor. ". . . Don't, Bertraine . . . you've killed too many people already . . ." she heard him saying, and his voice was deathly calm.

How could he be so calm?

Emile's hand was shaking; she heard the click of the safety-cock, felt the pressure as he impelled her forward watching as

Woodville backed away, his pistol still leveled.

When the shot rang out, she was surprised that she felt nothing, that blackness reached up and swallowed her into its dark maw.

Chapter Nine

"It was touch and go, Elise, and no mistake!" Noel told his sister with far more cheerfulness than he was really feeling. "But I must say, if Woodville hadn't had the idea that I was to go around to the back of that place and come through the kitchen into the passageway from behind, just in case, I daresay you would have been sticking your spoon in the wall right now!"

From the bed, his sister sighed. "Dr. Monro says that I have only a very slight scratch, and that he expects that in a few days I won't even know that it happened at all. But if you had not fired when you had, Noel, Emile would have killed me!" Her hand sought her brother's on the coverlet, and he squeezed it tightly.

"I'm just glad that Woodville had the foresight to take me into his confidence! Only think, Elise—if Emile had—" His voice trailed away.

"He was our friend, Noel . . . but Emile was always a gambler, you know that. I think even if he had had pots of money, he would have—"

Noel nodded. In a few seconds, his face brightened though. "I say, though, Elise, Woodville's a capital fellow! If only you could have seen him, laying out his plans to save you—by Jove, I never knew that the wind was blowing in that direction! You never said a word to me!"

Elise turned her head away.

Oblivious, her brother continued. "He was the most complete hand! Anyway, he says that I ain't cut out for the Foreign Office, and he's right. He says that he will speak to Uncle about buying me a commission in the army—and I think that's a capital idea! I have a notion that a pair of colors is exactly what I want, you know—no more of this being wrapped in cotton wool—"

"Noel, I think you're tiring Elise," Lady Charlotte suggested gently from the chair in the corner. "Dr. Monro says she's had quite a shock, and none of us must tease her too much yet. . . ."

Noel nodded. "But still, it was famous, Elise! Imagine, Woodville knew all along that Emile was planning to do me in and make off with you and the memorandum! Rather like one of those plays at Covent Garden! I wish you would see him—he and Lord Brandamore ought to be back from your opening exhibition by now. It's really too bad you couldn't attend! Uncle's as proud as punch of you, and telling all the world what a pair of heroes we are!"

"No," Elise said quietly. "I still do not want to see him!" She turned hollow eyes upon her brother and her friend. "Noel, Charlotte—what he will think of me when he sees that awful picture—oh, I could die! And I owe him my life! What a terrible wretch he will think me!"

Lady Charlotte rustled up from her chair and crossed to the bed, smoothing Elise's hair and patting her hand gently. "Dr. Monro told you that you must not excite yourself, Elise!" she commanded firmly. "Now please, do calm down!"

She shooed at Noel, who stood up, glad to be relieved of the duty of visiting an invalid. "Well, Elise, I'll drop in on you tomorrow, but you were a great gun to do what you did for me, and I won't forget it! From now on, I'm going to be as clean as a parson's cat!"

As he left the room, Lady Charlotte shook her head slightly, not believing a word of it.

Evidently, his sister did not either, for a faint smile flickered across her face. "I daresay his good resolutions shall last about a week, but, oh, Charlotte! Whatever shall I—"

"No, my love, you must be quiet! Dr. Monro

said that you must have absolute quiet! It will do you no good to test yourself!"

"But, oh! Whatever must he think? All of London will be there and they will see it, and they will talk—"

"Indeed they shall!" said a stern voice from the doorway, and both women turned their heads to see Mr. Woodville, immaculate in his evening clothes, filling up the doorway. There was a dark look upon his face, and something forbidding exuded from his bearing.

As he entered the room, he barely glanced at his stepmother. "You will leave us, if you please!" he barked.

Without a word, Charlotte scurried out the door, her skirts rustling, and Mr. Woodville faced Miss Pellerin.

She sat up slightly and drew the flounced sheets up about her neck, staring at him with wide, dark eyes.

Sternly, he placed his hands upon his hips and stared down at her, his fair, handsome face raking over hers. "Miss Pellerin," he began, "your portrait of Mephistopheles was without a doubt—"

She could not meet his gaze; her eyes dropped to the coverlet.

"—the most dreadful, impertinent and doubtless, thoroughly honest, piece of portraiture it has ever been my honor to behold!"

Unbelieving of what she had heard, Elise looked up.

A smile was lurking in his eyes as he sank to the side of the bed and grasped her hand tightly within his own. "Miss Pellerin, I know this is highly improper, but if you can find your way clear to forgiving me for allowing you to set yourself up as bait for the trap I cast about Emile Bertraine—who will fill the noose he intended for your brother very well, thanks to the confession he so thoughtfully penned for you to mail to me from your journey to Dover—"

Elise looked up again. "Can you forgive me for not believing you? For—for that odious portrait?"

"Odious! I bought it! For five hundred pounds! Your uncle drives a hard bargain, I must say!"

Elise could not help allowing a gurgle of laughter to escape from beneath the coverlet she held over her lips.

"Elise, what I want to ask you is—"

There was a scuffling sound at the doorway, and they both looked up. Undaunted, Mr. Woodville continued. "Elise, damme, will you marry me, or shall I continually be rescuing you from scrapes when you should be devoting your time to your art?"

"Christian!" she exclaimed, sitting upright just in time to be swept up into a breathless embrace that, in a most satisfactory manner, was crushing her against the white front of his dress waistcoat.

"I think I am ruining your cravat," she managed to murmur between kisses.

"Damn my waistcoat," Mr. Woodville said savagely, trying again.

At that moment, the door, inadequately closed, swung back to reveal the very interested personages of Lady Charlotte and Lord Brandamore.

Two pairs of interested eyes met two other pairs of equally interested eyes. "I say! Miss Pellerin, capital show of your canvases! Thought you might like to know that everyone tonnish was there—fired off very well, don't you know! Make you a fashion of your own! Daresay all the misses will be paintin' in oils soon—er, Woodville, ain't quite all the thing to be in a lady's bedroom, y'know! Might ask you what you're doing?"

"Proposing!" Mr. Woodville replied sardonically. "And what's more, Brandamore, if you're half the gentleman you say you are, you and that scatterbrained stepmother of mine might just consider a similar situation!"

And with those words, he rose and closed the door, turning to Elise with a devilish grin upon his face. "Now, my love, where were we?" he asked.

"I believe you were making violent love to me," Miss Pellerin, also smiling, answered demurely.

Outside the door, Lord Brandamore turned to Lady Charlotte. "Well, Charl'," he asked, slightly bemused. "You see what comes of tryin' to bring females into fashion! They get into dashed scrapes with spies and such like. Instead of makin' me exert myself, why don't you just marry me?"

"George, what a wonderful idea! Indeed, you are the cleverest man!" Lady Charlotte replied.

MASTER NOVELISTS

CHESAPEAKE·   CB 24163 $3.95
by James A. Michener

An enthralling historical saga. It gives the account of different generations and races of American families who struggled, invented, endured and triumphed on Maryland's Chesapeake Bay. It is the first work of fiction in ten years to be first on *The New York Times Best Seller List*.

THE BEST PLACE TO BE   PB 04024 $2.50
by Helen Van Slyke

Sheila Callaghan's husband suddenly died, her children are grown, independent and troubled, the men she meets expect an easy kind of woman. Is there a place of comfort? a place for strength against an aching void? A novel for every woman who has ever loved.

ONE FEARFUL YELLOW EYE   GB 14146 $1.95
by John D. MacDonald

Dr. Fortner Geis relinquishes $600,000 to someone that no one knows. Who knows his reasons? There is a history of threats which Travis McGee exposes. But why does the full explanation live behind the eerie yellow eye of a mutilated corpse?

8002

Buy them at your local bookstore or use this handy coupon for ordering.

COLUMBIA BOOK SERVICE (a CBS Publications Co.)
32275 Mally Road, P.O. Box FB, Madison Heights, MI 48071

Please send me the books I have checked above. Orders for less than 5 books must include 75¢ for the first book and 25¢ for each additional book to cover postage and handling. Orders for 5 books or more postage is FREE. Send check or money order only.

Cost $_____   Name_____

Postage_____   Address_____

Sales tax*_____   City_____

Total $_____   State_____ Zip_____

The government requires us to collect sales tax in all states except AK, DE, MT, NH and OR.

This offer expires 9/30/80

If you have your heart set on Romance, read
Coventry Romances

Each Coventry Romance is a love story rich in the customs and manners of England during the Regency, Georgian, Victorian, or Edwardian periods.

Beginning in November, there will be six new novels every month by such favorite authors as Sylvia Thorpe, Claudette Williams, and Rebecca Danton who will make you feel the elegance and grandeur of another time and place.

Look for the Coventry Romance displays wherever paperbacks are sold.

*Let Coventry give you
a little old-fashioned romance.*